Mirage

Book Two
Tru Exceptions Series

WRITTEN BY
Amanda Tru

Mirage
Copyright © 2012 by Amanda Tru

Cover design by Samantha Bayarr

Walker Hammond Publishers

ISBN-13: 978-0615629070 (Custom)
ISBN-10: 0615629075
Also available in ebook publication

PRINTED IN THE UNITED STATES OF AMERICA

Chapter 1

Rachel stared at the phone. It was going to ring any second. Dawson always called her at night when he was traveling. He'd never missed a night, not a single one. It's not like she insisted that he check in with her. He'd just started the habit of calling every night when he was away to check in and let her know he was okay.

The phone was silent. Rachel wasn't a worrier by nature, but, when your boyfriend is a top agent with Homeland Security and frequently works extremely dangerous cases, you tend to get a little concerned. While she had purposely never mentioned being afraid for him, Dawson had been intuitive and sweet enough to prevent much potential concern with a nightly update. Not that he ever told her anything about the cases he was working on. The man was like a high security vault when it came to his job. This fact aggravated Rachel to no end. She was curious, okay nosey, about Dawson's work, especially since she'd had a full dose of the danger involved six months ago when she'd become entangled in a terrorist plot involving a bomb in New York City. Rachel had escaped the encounter with her life, the knowledge that she had helped foil the plan and save lives, and one incredibly handsome Homeland Security agent as a boyfriend.

To her surprise, Dawson had joined her back in Montana, accepting a promotion that allowed him more flexibility. Although Dawson was now a supervisor, he still had to travel a lot more than Rachel had originally anticipated. She'd thought he'd be supervising the cases of other agents, not working so many himself.

Despite the fact that he was gone a lot and could never tell her anything about what he was working on, the last six months had been the best of Rachel's life. She knew, without a doubt, that she was absolutely, positively, completely head-over-heels in love with Dawson Tate.

Now if he would just call! The mute phone sat in its cradle blissfully ignorant of any task it was supposed to be performing. The red power light on the base was the only sign that it was even functioning. Rachel growled in frustration and flopped back on her bed. It was late, and she was already so tired from a long day of feeding cattle and checking fences in the Montana cold.

Dawson had never been this late in calling before. He had left early this morning. His flight had landed hours ago. The only thing she knew about this trip was that he was flying to Florida, which he seemed to do a lot lately. Florida's time zone was two hours later than Montana's. He should have already called her from his hotel and been in bed.

Rachel's exhaustion and frustration soon turned to anger. She was not the type of girl to wait by the phone for a guy to call, no matter what the circumstances. She sat up, grabbed the cordless phone off the cradle, and purposely pushed the buttons for Dawson's cell phone number. If he wasn't going to have the decency to call her and let her know that he was safe, then she was going to call him and voice her thoughts on the issue.

The call went through but went straight to voicemail, as if the phone was turned off. Rachel disconnected the call before the beep to leave a message. His phone would show her missed call whether or not she left a message.

Why would his phone be off? He never turned it off. He always had to be available for his job. Any conversation or activity could be interrupted at any time by Dawson's phone. And now it was off?

She suddenly felt a jolt of fear. It wasn't like Dawson not to call her, and it really wasn't like him to turn his phone off. In fact, she had never known him to do so. Rachel scooted off her bed and padded barefoot across the cold hardwood floor to her closet. Finding her coat, she rummaged around in the pocket for her own cell phone. Part of her didn't even know why she bothered. Dawson never called her on her cell phone at home. He knew she got terrible reception.

Dawson's phone, on the other hand, was almost like a star trek version of a cell phone; he got great reception wherever he was. Rachel knew the latest technology and the fact that it was a government issued and maintained phone had something to do with Dawson's stellar coverage. But, since she didn't have the option for *that* service provider, she simply had to continue with her rotten coverage and her slightly jealous hatred of Dawson's futuristic communication device.

Rachel's hand finally connected with the phone. She drew it out of the pocket and looked at it. No new messages. No missed calls.

Thoughtfully she took the cell phone back to bed and lay down. She had already showered and was in her most unflattering flannel pajamas. Her parents had gone to bed hours ago in their bedroom on the opposite side of the ranch house. Rachel laid both the cordless phone and her cell phone beside her on the bed.

There had to be a perfectly reasonable, safe answer for why Dawson hadn't called. Maybe he had lost his cell phone. Maybe something important had come up and he was tied up in a late night meeting.

But no matter how much she tried, no excuses shrank the stark fear lodged in the pit of her stomach. If Dawson had really been heading for a dangerous mission, surely he would have told her something or given her some kind of warning, even if he couldn't share the details, right?

The thoughts swirling around her head soon morphed into dreams. A man in a dark jacket stood a few feet away from Dawson, his extended hand holding a gun aimed directly at Dawson's head. Dawson was unarmed, helpless. Rachel could see the man's finger poised on the trigger. She screamed, but no sound came out. She tried to run to reach him, but something physically held her back. Her feet wouldn't move. The gun fired. Dawson fell as Rachel's screams echoed through the air and the entire scene dissolved before her eyes.

Now she was on a beach facing two figures caught in each other's arms as they stood in the foaming surf. Rachel moved forward, the sand warm on her bare feet as she was drawn like a magnet to the embracing couple. The man's face turned toward her. Dawson! He didn't seem to even notice Rachel's presence as his attention was completely focused on the beautiful brunette in his arms. He smiled, drawing her close once more and kissing her long and tenderly. A sob caught in Rachel's throat.

The first ring of a phone shattered the beach scene. Rachel's hand fumbled for the handset.

"Hello?" she managed, her voice still muddled with sleep.

"Hey, Rachel. It's Dawson. I'm sorry to wake you, Sweetheart, but I didn't want you to worry. I got redirected to New York. I'm so sorry I wasn't able to call you earlier, but I've been in an urgent meeting with Andrews. I couldn't call you sooner."

The simple sound of his voice blew away her anger and fear, leaving her weak and slightly speechless.

"I'm just glad to know you're okay," she finally said simply, deciding it would do no good to tell him how really scared she'd been.

"I need to let you get more sleep, but I'll call you in the morning and we can talk longer. Sleep well, Rachel. I love you."

At the sound of those three precious little words, Rachel bolted upright in bed. Her Dawson had never told her he loved her.

She looked around her bedroom, seeing the faint light of dawn breaking through the late winter sky and breaching the edges of the blue gingham curtains at her window. The two phones lay undisturbed on the mattress beside her. Rachel went from asleep to awake and panicking in a split second as two realizations hit her. One, it was morning. Two, Dawson had never called.

Chapter 2

The echo of their footsteps in the long hallway completely unnerved Rachel. Her heart was pounding, and she suddenly couldn't swallow the lump in her throat. What was she thinking? She had the sudden strong desire to turn around and run back down the hallway. But, no! She had come this far, she couldn't stop now.

When Rachel had woken up yesterday morning, she had immediately called her friend and Homeland Security agent, Kelsey Johnson. After doing some checking, more to humor Rachel than anything else, Kelsey had finally confirmed Rachel's worst fears. The agency couldn't locate him. Dawson was missing.

Kelsey had refused to give Rachel any information about Dawson, the case he'd been working on, or their strategy to find him. Quickly developing a desperate plan of her own, Rachel had immediately booked the next flight from Helena to Florida. Unfortunately, the only one available had been a red eye flight leaving that afternoon. It was maddening to Rachel to have to wait when she knew Kelsey and other DHS agents from the New York office had been able to take an immediate flight. But finally, after a stressful and sleepless night next to a snorer, Kelsey had picked Rachel up at the airport when her early morning flight had landed in Miami.

Now, walking down a long hallway to meet with Kelsey's boss, second thoughts bombarded Rachel. She had to be crazy to even be considering this plan.

"Rachel, you don't have to do this," Kelsey said, her quiet voice echoing. Rachel had met Kelsey and developed a friendship after the bomb incident in New York six months ago. Now, though, she really didn't need Kelsey giving voice to the doubts already inside her head. She needed her support.

"You're wrong, Kelsey," Rachel replied firmly. "I don't have a choice. I have to join Homeland Security."

"You do have a choice," Kelsey argued. "You just don't like the other option."

"You won't tell me anything about Dawson! He's been missing now over twenty-four hours! The only way I'll get any information is if I'm a member of the department."

"You're right, Rachel. I can't tell you anything about Dawson or his disappearance, but can't you just trust that we're doing everything we can to locate him? We are Homeland Security, after all. It's not like we're incompetent. You'll have to forgive me for saying this Rachel, but what makes you think that YOU can do a better job of finding him?

Rachel shut her eyes. Kelsey had paused in front of a door. Rachel turned to face her. "I don't think Homeland Security is incompetent, and I don't have any illusions about coming here and saving the day. But I can't sit home and do nothing, Kelsey!"

Rachel's eyes begged her to understand. Kelsey was petite and beautiful, resembling the Disney Princess Snow White more than a government agent. But, Rachel knew Kelsey was tough. If she couldn't convince her friend, she had no hope of convincing Kelsey's boss to let her join and participate in the investigation

"I hate to say this, Rachel, but you need to know. Our line of work is dangerous, and Dawson's cases are usually the worst. The bad guys he investigates won't waste time kidnapping a government agent and keeping him alive. If they thought Dawson was onto them, they would simply eliminate the problem. As you said, it's been over twenty-four hours. The chances of him being found alive..."

"I know, Kelsey. I know." Rachel closed her eyes, breathing a silent prayer.

Please, God, no! Let him be alive!

Looking once again at Kelsey, Rachel's eyes begged her friend to understand. "I have to try. Please. I have to at least try."

Kelsey's eyes searched Rachel's face, and then finally, she nodded. "Okay, Rachel. Just so you know what you're getting into. Andrews will let you join. He'll probably be very pleased with himself. He already extended you an offer months ago, and he doesn't do that lightly. But, you need to know what you're signing up for. He'll drive a hard bargain, and he usually gets his way. Be very sure that this is what you want, what you need to do. Get him to agree to let you in on the investigation before you sign anything. Then be careful to read every word. He'll hold you to every letter in a contract."

"Okay. Thank you, Kelsey. I'll be careful."

"Just to let you know, I'm supposed to come with you, but I won't be able to give you any advice or anything. I pretty much have to keep my mouth shut." Kelsey nodded to the door in front of them. "He's expecting us."

Rachel didn't give herself time to think. She knocked on the door, waited two seconds, and turned the door handle before her mind could even process what she was doing and try to stop her.

"Rachel Saunders! Come in, come in!" Andrews said cheerfully, looking up from the computer he had been focused on. Kelsey followed Rachel into the room and shut the door softly. Andrews stood, threw a pair of reading glasses on the desk, and came forward immediately to shake Rachel's hand.

"Miss Johnson tells me you're finally interested in joining us here at Homeland Security," he said with a friendly smile and a firm handshake.

"Yes, sir, I am," Rachel replied simply, hoping her nervousness wouldn't show in her voice.

"Have a seat." Andrews instructed. "I'd offer you something to drink, but I'm in unfamiliar territory here. The Drug Enforcement Agency and Homeland Security share offices here in Miami. They are both being kind enough to let those of us from New York barge in and set up a temporary camp, but I don't think that includes any of the usual amenities."

Rachel and Kelsey sat in the two chairs facing the desk. Andrews resumed his position behind it. Pressing his fingers together and bringing them to his lips in a thoughtful posture, Andrews studied Rachel silently. Rachel barely managed to keep from squirming under his scrutiny as her nervousness increased about tenfold.

Not knowing what else to do, Rachel held his gaze and returned his study. She had only seen Andrews once before. But since that had been right after the bomb had exploded and she and Dawson had barely escaped with their lives, she hadn't had the presence of mind to notice any details about the man, other than the fact that he was bald.

Now she made a more thorough inspection. He was tall, and Rachel guessed his age to be early fifties. His eyes were gray and intelligent. They weren't unkind, but Rachel thought they could be very intense and cutting if necessary. He wore a suit and looked as if he maintained an active lifestyle.

Dawson never talked about Andrews. He never talked about anything work-related. But from his attitude and a few comments Kelsey had made, Rachel had gathered that Andrews was a good boss but had extremely high expectations for his staff. He liked results and, although he appeared to have a laid-back attitude, it masked an intensity that had probably earned him his top position.

Finally, Andrews smiled, blinked, and shifted position, ending their staring contest. He began shuffling through papers on the desk, as if looking for something.

"Now, I'm curious, Rachel," Andrews said, as if his unsettling inspection had never happened. "Just so I know, which offer are we going to be discussing today? I sent you several with different benefits mentioned, so I need to know what compensation you're anticipating."

"Sir, I'm not sure what you're talking about," Rachel replied, completely mystified. "I only ever received one offer, and that was pretty informal. As I was getting on the plane to leave New York six months ago, Kelsey mentioned that you wanted to make me an offer to join Homeland Security. We didn't get into any particulars. She just said I'd be well compensated."

Andrews paused his work with the papers and once again stared at Rachel, but this time, Rachel witnessed that intense gaze firsthand.

"What do you mean you only received only one offer? I sent you multiple letters outlining formal offers for you to accept a position as an agent."

Rachel was lost. "Sir, I never received anything like what you're talking about. The only time a job with Homeland Security was ever mentioned to me was that once."

Andrews was silent, still staring at her. But Rachel noticed a slow red creeping up his neck.

"Tate!" he growled.

He looked like someone who had just realized he had been completely and thoroughly conned.

"Tell me, Miss Saunders, did you have any idea that your boyfriend was screening your mail?"

"I don't see how that's possible," Rachel replied, more than a little confused. "Dawson never touches the mail. I always have to give him anything that comes for him. Besides, he is travelling and out of town so much, there's no way he could intercept my mail."

"Is this your address?" Andrews asked, handing Rachel a sheet of paper.

"No, it isn't. This address is for a post office box in Helena. All of my mail is sent to my physical address at my parents' ranch."

Andrews slammed his fist on the desk, making Rachel jump.

"That's how he did it then. He must have changed the information on the file we have for you, listing a post office box he created to intercept my offers. I tried to get your email address as well, but he said you didn't have internet at the ranch. I also called for you once at the phone number listed under your parents' name. Tate answered and said you weren't available. He said your dad had had a heart attack, and, as you were busy with him, the phone was not the best way to reach you."

"We do have internet at the ranch. It's spotty at times, but we do have it. My dad did have a heart attack, but that was over two years ago!"

Andrews shook his head. "I knew from your file that your dad had a heart attack a while ago, but the way Dawson said it, I thought he'd had another one. I can't believe I was so easily duped by my own agent."

"I still don't understand," Rachel said uneasily. "Why would Dawson go to all of that trouble to prevent me from getting your letters?"

"That's something you'll have to ask him. All I know is that when I initially mentioned wanting to extend you an offer, he was very opposed. He said he didn't think you would be a good match for the agency. I tried to question him further, but he wouldn't really share his reasons."

Instant anger boiled in Rachel. How dare he interfere like that! Coupled with the anger was hurt and insecurity about Dawson's motives. Did Dawson really think her so incompetent that she couldn't handle being an agent? He'd always said he liked that she was so strong and capable. But now she doubted those words. What did he really think of her?

"Don't worry," Andrews was saying. Rachel tried to focus on his words. "When Dawson shows up, I'll take care of this issue."

As far as Rachel was concerned, Andrews was going to have to get in line behind her!

"Alright," Andrews continued. "Since you obviously don't know about the offers I extended, I can just go over the benefits of each one and then you can decide what you want to do."

"With all due respect, sir, I'd rather not," Rachel said firmly. "As angry as I am with Dawson Tate right now, the fact remains that he is missing. I would like to assist in finding him sooner rather than later. Would it be okay if we just went with the very last offer you made? I'm guessing, since you said you made multiple offers, that the very last one was probably the best."

Andrews grinned. "Smart girl. That's what we'll do then."

Andrews located the right set of papers, positioned his glasses, and began explaining everything the contract entailed. Rachel tried to focus, but couldn't. Her thoughts vacillated between fury at Dawson for his behavior to sheer panic at the knowledge that he was missing.

When Andrews paused momentarily to locate the final section of the contract, Rachel quickly inserted the one question burning in her mind.

"Will I be permitted to work at finding Dawson?"

"Yes, you will." Andrews replied, peering over the glasses perched on his nose. "Normally there is no way I would allow someone romantically or even emotionally involved with an agent anywhere close to a case he was involved in. Emotions tend to cause costly mistakes in our business. However, I have my reasons for making an exception for you. Your first assignment as an agent will be to find Dawson Tate."

Rachel nodded. "Thank you. I appreciate that."

"However," Andrews continued. "I cannot allow you to join Homeland Security for just this case. I'm sure you understand. I need to have some kind of commitment from you. After we find Dawson, I cannot allow you to simply quit. I feel it very reasonable and, almost lenient, to ask that you sign a one-year contract. Typically, I would insist on a longer time frame. We invest a lot into our agents and can't have one quitting after just a year. But, this isn't really a normal circumstance. You will not have had the training other agents have had prior to signing a contract like this. In a sense, you won't have gotten your feet wet and made sure this is really what you want. I understand that. I feel a year's time will give you the experience you need to be more comfortable with a more permanent decision and give us the information we need to determine if you are a good investment. In a year, we will reassess and have the option to renew this contract."

A year was scary, especially since she didn't really know what her new job would entail. What was she going to do about the ranch? Her dad depended on her to help. What would she do if she had to travel like Dawson, or worse, was based out of New York?

On the other hand, Andrews' offer sounded more than fair and reasonable. She pushed all of her questions and fears aside. She would figure everything out later, after she knew Dawson was safe. Right now, she had to do this.

"That sounds reasonable," she found herself responding. "I am willing to commit for a full year."

A couple minutes later, Andrews handed Rachel a pen and pointed to the line requiring her signature. She placed the pen on the paper. She got kicked in the ankle. Hard. She darted a look over at Kelsey, who remained silent and serene, acting as if she had never thought of delivering such a blow. Though she hadn't made a sound throughout

Rachel's entire conversation with Andrews, Rachel now received Kelsey's message loud and clear.

Obediently, she shuffled back through the papers, trying to skim each section hurriedly. But her mind couldn't focus. She read the words, but they held no meaning. Mostly she just tried to put on enough of a show to satisfy her friend.

But, within about two minutes, she couldn't take it anymore. She knew as soon as she signed these papers, she would be given the information about Dawson and be able help find him. He could, even now, be injured or in danger. Every minute could be counting down his life.

Quickly, she turned to the last page.

Please, God, help me not to be making a mistake!

With a quick flourish, she signed her name.

Andrews instructed her to sign a few more places. Rachel felt the disapproval emanating from Kelsey. Apparently, she hadn't taken long enough to read the contract. Finally, Andrews gathered up the papers.

"Congratulations, Rachel Saunders. You are now officially an agent. Let me be the first to welcome you to the Department of Homeland Security."

Rachel faked a smile and shook the extended hand of her new boss.

She had done it! Now she could work on finding Dawson. She should feel relieved, proud even. So why did she instead feel as if she had just signed her life away?

Chapter 3

"Now that we have the business side of things taken care of, I can fill you in on Agent Tate," Andrews said. "The problem is, we don't know much. Dawson Tate is probably the best agent I have, but he's also an enigma to just about everyone here in the department. He's extremely independent, preferring to work alone. He also doesn't always follow the rules. In short, he's completely disappeared and left us virtually no clues on how to find him."

"But what about the case he was working on?" Rachel said. "Surely his disappearance is connected with what he was working on. Where are the case files? His notes?"

Andrews grimaced. "There are none. Like I said, Dawson is independent and doesn't follow the rules. It's partially my fault. I don't insist on the paperwork and documentation with him that I do with other agents. He gets results. At the end of the day, it doesn't matter to me how he does it. All I know is that when Tate has figured a case out, he comes to me with completed paperwork, impeccable documentation, and hard, solid evidence. Up until that point, he doesn't talk, and I don't ask questions."

"But you're his boss! Surely you knew what he was working on, even if you didn't insist on paperwork."

"I do know what assignment I gave him, but I don't know which direction he's gone from there or what progress he has made. All I know is that for the last six months he's continued investigating the terrorist ring from the attempted New York City bombing."

"The terrorist ring? I thought everything was taken care of and the case was closed after so many terrorists were apprehended that night."

"No," Andrews said with a smile. "Tate may have led you to believe that to make you feel better, but that night was only the beginning of our investigation. These things usually take years to officially close."

Rachel felt like a naive fool. Of course, now it made sense. There was no way a massive plot like they experienced could be investigated so quickly and tied up so nice and neatly.

"Specifically, I tasked Tate with investigating the American angle," Andrews continued. "We had strong reason to suspect that the terrorist ring wasn't an entirely overseas operation. Dawson was trying to figure out possible American accomplices in the terrorist ring and the failed plot. He was given a list of suspects. But, beyond that, I don't know who he zeroed in on."

At Andrews' words, several things seemed to shift into place and suddenly make sense to Rachel. "Of course! I remember being surprised that some of the terrorists we talked with had no accent. They spoke like Americans!"

"Exactly right," Andrews confirmed. "There were too many apprehended Americans for us to feel completely comfortable with the explanation that they had been hired to assist a group of overseas Muslim extremists."

Rachel was quiet, processing the information. So all they knew was Dawson's case description. They had none of the details of his investigation, or even who he had been investigating. Obviously, the fact that he was missing showed that he had found something and probably gotten too close. But, now they had no way of following up on his leads or even tracking him.

Rachel suddenly felt very frustrated. How was she going to find Dawson if she had no idea where to look? Maybe Kelsey was wrong about Dawson's case being in good hands. It was sounding more and more like they were incompetent!

"I still can't believe you've never insisted on knowing what he was doing," Rachel said, ignoring the internal warning and venting a little of her frustration her boss's direction. "It seems like too much of a risk because of exactly this scenario. An agent working an undisclosed case goes missing, and nobody even knows what he was working on. Plus, from a standpoint of the department, all of Dawson's work will be completely lost if he's not found."

"You're right, Rachel. Tate and I have discussed those very issues. I was not comfortable with his methods from either standpoint of his well-being or the best interest of the department. The problem is that Tate trusts no one, including me. He works on extremely dangerous, highly classified investigations. He's always overly suspicious about potential large level conspiracies involving high level positions. You have to understand that with the kind of terrorist networking he unravels, such suspicions are not unwarranted. While I usually give him assignments and know the general case, he doesn't update me until he has completed it. That doesn't mean he doesn't keep case files. His notes are so specific, I'm sure he keeps them. I just don't know where. The only reason I was ever okay with his secrecy was that he has always assured me that he had a failsafe, a backup plan so that we would have the necessary information from his case should anything happen to him."

"A failsafe?" Rachel questioned. "What did he mean?"

"Well, since, he became involved with you, I've assumed that failsafe was you."

"Me?" Rachel replied, thoroughly shocked. "Why would you think that? Dawson has never given me any information about his work. Ever. I know absolutely nothing about what he was working on. His failsafe must be something else."

"Not necessarily," Andrews said. "Just because you don't realize it, doesn't mean Tate hasn't given you the information we need. You just may not even be aware of it. This is one of the reasons I need you on this case. If Tate trusts anybody, he trusts you. He knows how smart and capable you are. If he needed to leave important information, he'd leave it with you."

Rachel was searching her memory and drawing a complete blank. This had just been a normal trip for Dawson. He certainly hadn't acted or said anything differently. How could she convince Andrews that Dawson NEVER discussed anything related to work with her? And, obviously, he didn't think much of her intelligence or capabilities if he hadn't thought she'd be a good agent.

"Tell me, Rachel," Andrews continued. "You obviously don't think Dawson left anything of significance with you. But, did you happen to go through any of his personal things before you came?"

Rachel didn't answer. She felt a slow blush start spreading through her face.

"Good girl!" Andrews laughed. What did you find?

Rachel still felt embarrassed about the fact that she had gone through Dawson's things, but she hadn't been able to stop herself. Six months ago, Rachel's parents had offered Dawson the use of their guest cottage in exchange for his help around the ranch when he was in town. It really had been the perfect arrangement, allowing Dawson to come and go as needed and spend time with Rachel, while allowing Rachel and her dad to get caught up on some bigger projects with Dawson's help.

Before his first trip from Montana, Dawson had unceremoniously plopped a ring of keys in front of her, explaining that he was giving her a copy of all of his keys in case she ever needed them while he was away. A curious person by nature, she was very proud of the fact that she hadn't ever gone snooping before. She hadn't even been inside the guest house since Dawson had moved in.

After her morning phone call with Kelsey, Rachel had booked her flight, but the earliest she could leave was late afternoon. So she'd ended up having several hours to feel helpless and go completely crazy. Desperate to find some clue about Dawson's disappearance or the case he'd been working on, she had gone to their guest house and made a thorough inspection of everything belonging to Dawson.

Even though she knew Dawson had purposely left her his keys so she could access his things if she had the need, she had still felt self-conscious about being in his place. Now she felt even worse about having to thoroughly confess her nosiness.

"I didn't really find anything that seemed important," Rachel said, remembering how startlingly clean and organized Dawson's place was and how disappointed she'd been that she had found very few of his personal effects.

"Then humor me and tell me what you found that seemed unimportant."

Rachel gave up on her pride and spoke as she rummaged around in the bag she'd brought with her. "Dawson stays in my parent's guest house at the ranch. It really resembled more of a hotel room than a guy's personal space. It was very organized and held almost nothing personal of Dawson's. There wasn't really anything to find. It was as if he purposely didn't leave anything in case I might find it. As if he knew that somehow, someday, I would go through his things."

Rachel found the 3 by 5 inch white card she had been looking for in her purse. She handed it across the desk to Andrews. "I found this in his top drawer."

To Rachel's embarrassment, Andrews read the card aloud, "'Stop snooping, Montana. If you need to know something, I'll tell you. Trust me.'"

Andrews leaned back and let loose deep bellows of laughter. "I take it you're 'Montana,'" he finally asked, even though he obviously already knew the answer.

Rachel nodded. "Dawson has called me 'Montana' since the day we met."

That triggered another round of laughter. Although Kelsey had the decency not to laugh, Rachel could see that her eyes were sparkling with suppressed amusement.

Finally, Andrews' laughter died down. "That's typical Dawson Tate. Always two steps ahead of everyone else! But, I still don't think that note means that you aren't the failsafe. He didn't know when you'd find that note. He was just counting on enjoying it immensely when you did!"

He handed her back the card, saying, "So did you find anything else?"

After his reaction to her last find, Rachel was very reluctant to show him anything else, but she obediently looked through her purse once more.

When Rachel had found Dawson's note, it had made her angry and embarrassed, as if she'd been caught red handed in a crime she had never intended to commit. The nerve of the man! She had then begun 'snooping' with renewed enthusiasm. If Dawson had expected her to look through his stuff, then she figured she may as well do a thorough, satisfying job of it. She'd looked under the bed, beneath the pillows on his bed, and behind every picture frame on the wall. Searching through the keys on her key ring, she found the one to open the gun cabinet and searched there too.

All of her searching had turned up nothing. She'd only found one other personal item, and she was sure it had nothing to do with his case or disappearance. As her hand connected with the piece of paper in her bag, she pulled it out and handed it to Andrews in one smooth motion before she could change her mind. By this point, she knew her face was flaming, but she didn't have a choice. She was more than willing to suffer extreme embarrassment if only on the off-chance that the paper might provide some clue to find Dawson.

"I found it hidden in a pocket in the back of Dawson's Bible," Rachel explained.

This time, Andrews was quiet and serious as he examined the paper.

It was a list. A list all about Rachel. In one column was listed "What Rachel Likes." The other column was labeled "What Rachel Dislikes." In the "like" column was listed things like Dove Chocolate, cheesecake, strawberries, daisies, her favorite music, and even details like her favorite brand of jeans and toothpaste, and the fact that she liked vanilla lotion and any movie with Matthew Maconahay in it. In the "Dislike" column was listed broccoli, hot dogs, diet soda, hip hop, the names of several restaurants, and several obscure details like the fact that she'd eat eggs scrambled but no other way, and the fact that she had a strong aversion to facial hair on men.

At the bottom of the page was a third list titled: 'Gift Ideas for Rachel.' Under the heading was listed everything from technology like a Kindle and iPad to boots. Some very specific jewelry was listed, including a necklace with her birthstone. Books and a few random items she had mentioned in passing, like a touch activated lamp for her bedroom were also listed. He'd even written tickets to a Broadway show with several top examples given as possibilities. Last on the list was a Walther 9 mm gun.

When Rachel had read the paper, her heart had melted. What a sweet thing to do! Dawson listened to her! He cared about what she said and the things she liked and disliked. He cared enough that he wanted to be sure he remembered them and got her perfect, thoughtful gifts. The sweet man knew she liked daisies, but also knew she wanted a gun! Even if Dawson had never said the words, this was proof that he loved her, right?

Of course, she had also considered the possibility that Dawson had expected her to find this, but she doubted it. It had been hidden in difficult-to-find inner pocket of his Bible.

"Could be a code of some kind," Andrews mused. "But I doubt it. Even so, I'll have some of our experts take a look and see what they think."

Great, now the entire department will know everything about me, including the fact that I hate facial hair! Rachel thought with humiliation. How long would it take for the relentless teasing to start? It wasn't like she could prevent it from happening.

"I would like to have the list back when they're done," she said quietly.

"Of course." Andrews responded.

She really appreciated that, this time, Andrews was all business. Not even a gleam of humor showed in his eyes.

"I think we're done here for now. End recording," Andrews said, reaching inside his suit jacket and pushing some kind of button.

At Rachel's questioning look, he explained. "Sorry, I guess I should have told you sooner. I make a habit of recording my conversations with agents, especially when I give them new assignments. My memory of details isn't as good as it used to be. This way, I can hold both the agent and myself accountable. I typically give any tapes to my administrative assistant and give her instructions as to what, if anything I want transcribed. The information is then put in a secure location in case it is ever needed and most recordings are usually destroyed within 24 hours. I was already recording some dictation when you arrived, so I just left it going."

Andrews' explanation made sense, but Rachel couldn't help but uneasily wonder what parts of her conversation with him were destined to be transcribed and placed in a permanent record.

Kelsey's phone beeped. She answered and listened a moment. Hanging up, her eyes met Andrews' and she started to stand.

"Go ahead, Agent Johnson. We're done. I'm going to take Saunders to meet the other agent I've assigned to work with her on Dawson's disappearance–Garrett Matthews."

Kelsey's eyes flew wide. She opened her mouth as if to say something, but then she must have changed her mind, pursing her lips together tightly and turning for the door.

"I'll catch up with you in a few minutes," she said instead.

Rachel followed as Andrews exited the room as well. They turned down the long hallway, the opposite direction from Kelsey.

"I'm sure you noticed Agent Johnson's reaction when I mentioned Garrett Matthews," Andrews said conversationally as they walked. "She probably doesn't like the idea of me throwing you directly into the fire."

Chapter 4

Though he and Rachel were the only ones in the hallway, Andrews spoke quietly, "Garrett Matthews and Dawson Tate don't historically have a good relationship. Plainly put, they dislike each other. My personal opinion is that they are too similar and too competitive with each other to get along. But it's not just that. Matthews is Tate intensified. He can be very rough around the edges. He says exactly what he thinks and doesn't get along with a lot of people here in the department. Johnson was probably wondering about my wisdom in assigning Matthews to investigate Tate's disappearance. The short answer is that Matthews is a fantastic agent, second only to Tate himself. Despite his personal feelings, Matthews will give his all for this case. He may have a difficult attitude at times, but his sense of integrity and honor won't allow him to do otherwise. He is the absolute best for this job. You just need to be aware that, like

Tate, he doesn't like partners. He will not be easy to work with."

"I understand," Rachel replied. "I'm sure I can handle it."

Andrews paused in front of a set of large double doors at the end of the hall. He turned to Rachel, his gaze intense. "There's one more thing. I made exceptions on many levels for you to join the department and work this case. Now you have to earn it. You're going to have to be tough and prove to everyone that you deserve to be here."

Rachel's sense of dread increased as Andrews spoke.

"There's already been a rumor circulating that I'm hiring Dawson Tate's girlfriend as an agent to help with the investigation. Unfortunately, they know nothing about you. Kelsey Johnson is probably the only other agent who knows the details of your involvement in preventing the New York terrorist attack. As far as everyone else knows, you're just Tate's girlfriend, you have no experience, and you haven't been required to go through all of the training and other demands placed on every other agent in the department. They already resent you. If I try to defend you and praise your qualifications, it will only increase the suspicion and resentment. There's only one option: you have to prove yourself.

Be tough, Rachel. Be the incredible hero from six months ago in New York. It's the only way you're going to earn respect and fit in here."

Momentary panic gripped Rachel. She fully understood what her boss was saying. But, she was just a girl from Montana. How could she ever hope to hold her own in a group of highly trained government agents, and an extremely irascible one in particular. Dawson had adapted to Montana ranch life like a duck to water. She seriously doubted that she would be able to fit into his world as well as he had fit into hers.

Rachel was aware of Andrews watching her closely, as if monitoring her reaction. Suddenly, steel determination flowed like liquid through her veins, replacing the fear. She would find a way to prove herself. She had to.

"I understand, sir," she said. "I won't disappoint you."

Andrews' eyes sparkled. "Thatta girl. I know you won't disappoint me. I've had a gut feeling about you since I found out about what happened in New York. That's why I hired you. I believe you're going to be invaluable to this case and to the department in general. Rachel Saunders, you're going to make a fantastic agent."

Rachel was humbled and more than a little intimidated by Andrews' expectations of her. But she didn't have time to think about it.

Andrews opened the door and led the way into a large open room filled with desks and people. It resembled what a police precinct looks like in all the detective shows on TV. Andrews walked over to a desk in the center of the room where a man was sitting going through a bunch of files. The man had dark brown hair and a chiseled face.

"Garrett Matthews," Andrews called as they came near.

Intense gray eyes shot up from looking at the files. His tall, athletic frame unfolded itself from the seat.

Great, Rachel thought sarcastically. *The agent with a bad attitude would have to be drop-dead gorgeous!*

Andrews spoke, "I need to introduce you to your partner on this case, Matthews. I expect…"

"You've got to be kidding me," Matthews interrupted. "Is this her? Is this his girlfriend? Come on, Andrews, you know I work alone. And you really can't expect me to find Tate while babysitting *her*!"

Andrews' mouth formed a grim line, and his eyes flashed his annoyance. "I expect you to do your job and follow orders, Matthews! You will give her all the information and include her in every aspect of this investigation. She is your partner in every way. Do I make myself clear? I have reason to believe she is uniquely qualified to assist in finding Dawson Tate."

"Understood, sir," Matthews replied, somewhat reluctantly. "But if I may…" he turned to face Rachel raking her up and down with his eyes. "May I ask what exactly your 'unique qualifications are?" he sneered, his tone full of acidic sarcasm.

What a jerk! Rachel had the strongest urge to wipe that sneer right off his face. Well, maybe… Remembering Andrews' warning, Rachel shot a glance his direction. He had a gleam in his eyes and gave a small, almost imperceptible nod.

Ignoring Matthews' question, Rachel extended her right hand to him. "It's nice to meet you, Agent Matthews. I'm Rachel Saunders."

Matthews eyed Rachel's hand like it was covered in filth, but he finally, reluctantly extended his own to meet hers.

Rachel clasped his hand firmly. Before he had time to blink, Rachel lifted their clasped hands and spun under it. His right arm now firmly twisted the wrong direction, she simultaneously hit his shoulder with her left hand while planting a hard kick to the back of his calf. It was all one fluid motion. The tall man completely dropped, hitting the floor hard.

His breath knocked out of him. He lay flat on his back with the heel of Rachel's boot positioned over his throat. He stared up at Rachel, who still held his right hand in an uncomfortable hold.

"I'm sorry, but I guess that's really all the qualifications I have," Rachel said sweetly.

Still out of breath, Matthews looked up, a new respect in his eyes. "And what… did you say your name was?"

Rachel smiled, removed her boot from his neck, readjusted her grip on his hand to a more comfortable position, and helped him up off the floor.

"Rachel," she replied. "Rachel Saunders."

Before Matthews could respond, they heard the hollow sound of someone clapping. Soon, that lone sound was joined by more and more. Rachel turned around to find Andrews grinning broadly and a roomful of government employees on their feet applauding.

She blushed to the roots of her hair.

Eventually, the applause died down and people returned to their work. Kelsey appeared at Andrews' elbow.

"Sir, I really need to talk to you. There have been some developments."

"On Tate's case? Well, go ahead, these two need to know as well, since they're in charge of the investigation."

"Sir, I'm not sure Rachel needs to hear this. Maybe we could find an office somewhere…"

"Tell us the news, Johnson," Andrews said impatiently. "Agent Saunders is on the case, and that includes every aspect. End of discussion."

Kelsey took a deep breath. "We received a call from the Miami Police Department. There's been a missing person's report filed for Dawson Tate."

Andrews looked confused. "Who reported him missing? His parents? They live in Florida, right?"

"No, they didn't file it," Kelsey replied grimly. "It was his fiancé."

Chapter 5

Rachel had to have heard wrong. His fiancé? Dawson didn't have a fiancé.

Matthews whistled and shook his head in shock.

Andrews darted a glance at Rachel, then addressed Kelsey. "So you're saying a woman claiming to be Dawson Tate's fiancé reported him missing? Who is this woman?"

"Her name is Vanessa Riley. I remember Dawson mentioning a Vanessa a few years ago. She was his girlfriend at the time. I think they even went to high school or college together. I can't remember. But my understanding was that they had broken up a while ago."

Andrews turned to Rachel.

She was numb. There had to be some mistake.

"Her name sounds familiar. Has Dawson ever mentioned Vanessa Riley to you?" he asked Rachel

"No. I knew he had an ex girlfriend in Florida, but I didn't know her name. There's no way she's his fiancé, though. There must be some mistake."

"Regardless, we need to talk to her and find out what she knows. Do you know where she is right now, Johnson?"

"The police still have her at the station. They recognized Dawson's name from the info we sent them, and they contacted us immediately. The precinct is ten minutes away. I'll call and tell them we're on our way."

"Good. The three of you go talk to her, and then get back to me. Understand?" Andrews was looking at Rachel. She knew he was wordlessly asking if she could handle this.

"Of course," she responded.

Rachel knew Dawson. There was no way he was engaged to someone else. He loved her, even if he'd never said the words. She would gladly go and clear up this misunderstanding with whoever this Vanessa Riley was.

Fifteen minutes later, the three agents were being escorted to a windowless room.

"One of us should watch from the one-way glass and not go inside," Kelsey said. "We don't know how much she knows about Dawson's real job or activities. We don't want her feeling overwhelmed or getting suspicious."

Both Kelsey and Matthews looked at Rachel expectantly, but she pretended ignorance. There was no way she was volunteering to sit this one out.

Kelsey sighed. "I guess I'll go take a spot behind the window. You two are lead on this, after all."

Matthews held open the door for Rachel and she walked into the small room. She felt sick to her stomach the second she saw Vanessa Riley. She was beautiful. She had soft brunette hair and brown eyes. Her features had a somewhat exotic look about them. Everything from her expertly highlighted hair to her jewelry and designer clothing screamed money.

Rachel had sat down in a chair across the table from Vanessa before she even processed that the woman wasn't alone. An older man with thinning gray hair sat beside her. By his suit and air of confidence, Rachel guessed that he was either an important man of some kind or that he at least thought he was important. Was he her lawyer?

"You must be Vanessa Riley," Matthews said, extending his hand with a friendly smile.

Did he actually have a nice guy side?

"Yes," she replied. "And this is my father, John Riley."

"And you are?" John Riley asked gruffly.

"I'm Garrett Matthews and this is Rachel Saunders. We are the detectives who have been assigned to find Dawson Tate," Matthews replied smoothly.

"I just can't believe this is happening!" Vanessa said, her long-lashed eyes tearing up. "Do you have any leads on finding him?"

"That's why we need to talk to you," Matthews said. "We need to ask you a few questions, if you don't mind."

"Of course." Vanessa replied dabbing at her eyes with a fancy lacy handkerchief.

"When was the last time you saw Mr. Tate?"

"I actually haven't seen Dawson for about two weeks. He owns and operates a company that specializes in elite security. He travels a lot. He flew back here the day before yesterday. His flight arrived in the afternoon, and he called me about 5:00. I can look at my cell phone to tell you the exact time. He was supposed to come to our house later that evening to finalize the last minute details for our engagement party. He never came, and he never called. At first, I thought something had just come up with his business. That's happened before. But the longer I didn't hear from him, the more concerned I was. I've tried over and over to call his cell phone, but it goes straight to voicemail. That never happens. Dawson always keeps his phone on. Yesterday evening Dad started using some of his connections to try to locate him. When we still hadn't heard or found anything this morning, I insisted we come first thing and file a missing persons report."

Both Rachel and Matthews had a notebook in front of them. As Vanessa spoke, Rachel pretended to take notes, but was too absorbed in her every word.

"And do you know if Dawson had any enemies? Anyone who might hold a grudge?"

"There's no one. I suppose in Dawson's line of work he doesn't always encounter the best sorts of people. I know he's been in dangerous situations before and worked for people who needed some pretty extreme security, but he's certainly never mentioned any enemies. He's a rather private person and doesn't talk about work much."

"I'm sorry, Miss Riley," Matthews said. "But I have to ask this. Is there any reason Dawson might want to disappear? Did you have an argument? Had he seemed unhappy lately?"

Matthews was good. Rachel knew what he was doing. He was expertly asking questions and guiding the conversation to get the information they needed, but he was doing it in a way that would never arouse suspicion about the probable cause of Dawson's disappearance. They were just the expected questions, normal for a situation like this, some of which he probably asked to deliberately throw Vanessa and her father off the truth. They obviously didn't know anything about Dawson's involvement with Homeland Security, and Matthews intended to keep it that way.

Rachel knew she was going to have to speak up and do the same thing if she was going to get the answers she needed. She had to prove herself. She had to remain stoic and seemingly detached no matter what Vanessa answered. She had to compartmentalize. She could fall apart later when no one was looking.

Vanessa's eyes filled with tears at Matthews' question. "No. Dawson and I were happy—we *are* happy. We haven't had any arguments. We are very much in love. We're getting married and making plans. We're both so excited."

Rachel jumped in before she could even process the meaning of Vanessa's words. "How long have you known Dawson Tate, Miss Riley. Is it possible that his disappearance could be tied to something further in his past, before you knew him?"

Vanessa shook her head. "Dawson and I have known each other for what seems like forever.

There's absolutely nothing in his past this could be tied to, and I should know. We went to the same high school and started dating in college. We've had our ups and downs for a very long time. We even broke up for several years at one point. Then, six months ago, Dawson called me, and we reconnected. This time when we got back together, we knew it was real. There was no backing out. We'd tried being apart, and it just hadn't worked. We both knew we would get married. We've known each other for so long, that neither one of us saw the purpose in a long engagement. Our wedding is in six weeks. Our engagement party is scheduled for tonight. What am I going to tell everyone?"

Vanessa softly cried into her handkerchief. Her father reached over protectively and rubbed her back.

Rachel realized she wasn't breathing. *Compartmentalize!* she ordered herself firmly. *Put it in a different part of the brain!* Vanessa wasn't talking about *her* Dawson. There was no way. Rachel and Dawson had just met and gotten together six months ago. There was no possible way he would pursue a relationship with Vanessa at the same time.

"I think we should take Dawson's disappearance public," John Riley said firmly.

"Somebody might have seen him or know something. I'm willing to offer a sizeable reward for any information leading to Dawson Tate's whereabouts."

"Let's wait on that for now, Mr. Riley," Matthews said smoothly. "At the moment, we have no idea why Dawson has disappeared. It could be for the simple reason of kidnapping for ransom. If you go public, that could complicate matters and put his life in danger. The best thing is just to sit tight and wait."

Mr. Riley grimaced, looking at his daughter with concern. "I'm a very well-known and successful businessman. If somebody was looking to get money from me, this would be the way to do it."

"What am I going to do?" Vanessa was moaning again brokenly.

"For now, you're going to do nothing," Matthews said. "You can't do anything until we have more information about what is going on. You'll have to go through with your engagement party and pretend that everything is just fine. Explain that Dawson was called away on an unexpected emergency. You could even make a joke that he assures you he's at least eighty percent sure that he will make it to the wedding. Then you wait until you get a ransom call or we have more information."

With full lips trembling, Vanessa nodded. "But what about Dawson's parents? I haven't had the heart to tell them yet. But they'll be at the party tonight. They know me well enough that they'll know something is wrong. Shouldn't I at least tell them?"

"We'll leave that decision up to you," Matthews said.

Rachel heard Matthews' response, but it was as if it was echoing from a different room. Vanessa's words were like nails being driven into her heart. She could no longer deny the truth. For while Vanessa seemed close to Dawson's parents, Rachel had never even met them.

When Rachel had mentioned wanting to meet them, Dawson had always changed the subject or had excuses: they were really busy or he just wanted to wait for the perfect time. Now she understood. A guy would never introduce his parents to his fake girlfriend, only the real one. Now she knew which one she was. She just didn't know why.

The conversation was over. She knew there wasn't any more information they needed from Vanessa right now. And, she knew she had to get out of there. Fast.

As if she were listening to someone else speak, she heard her own voice speaking calmly. "We'd like to get your contact information, Miss Riley. We'll call you when we find anything. We also may have to ask you more questions if needed."

"Certainly," she replied, writing the information on the notebook paper Rachel handed her. "I'll gladly do anything I can to help find Dawson."

After following Vanessa and John Riley out, Rachel and Matthews rejoined Kelsey.

Kelsey immediately focused on Rachel. "Rachel, are you okay?"

Rachel barely maintained control of her emotions as her friend's eyes probed her. Matthews was looking at her as well, as if expecting her to completely fall apart. And, oh, how she wanted to fall apart! But she couldn't. In that moment she accomplished one of the most difficult things she'd ever had to do. She stuffed all her hurt and anger in an imaginary bottle and sealed it. She swallowed the burning knot in her throat, kept her breathing regular, and refused to surrender to tears. It was sheer torture. But she kept control.

"Of course I'm okay," she replied, acting as if there was no reason for her to not be just fine. "But I really think we need to investigate both John and Vanessa Riley."

"And why is that?" Matthews asked. "Other than the fact that she is the fiancé of your so-called boyfriend."

Rachel glared at him. "For starters, I would like to know why nobody else in the department knew about Vanessa Riley either. Everyone Dawson worked with thought he was dating me. Seems a little bizarre. I would like to find out why and if it had any bearing on the case he was working. It also seems strange that the Rileys know nothing of his real job. Obviously, Dawson lied to me, but he was not completely truthful with her either. I think verifying their story is a good idea regardless of the circumstances. Finally, John Riley claimed he used his resources to try to find Dawson last night. I know that Dawson probably covered his tracks well, but I still find it strange that a man who seems as wealthy and influential as John Riley was not able to use his contacts and a very targeted effort to discover that Dawson Tate was actually a Homeland Security agent."

Matthews had the decency to look impressed with Rachel's analysis. "Very well put. I had thought of some of those same things. Let's head back to headquarters and get started."

Back at their borrowed home base, Kelsey left to report to Andrews and do some background checking on the Rileys while Rachel and Matthews set to work back at the desk in the large room where she had met him. Matthews thought it would be good to develop a timeline of Dawson's activities on the day he went missing. Rachel started constructing the timeline on a large whiteboard while Matthews worked the computer locating information such as Dawson's exact flight arrival time, bank records showing his transactions, and even his cell phone records.

They hadn't been working long when Kelsey came back.

"So far, everything about the Rileys' story is accurate. Andrews says that in some other cases, Dawson has used this same front of owning a security company. As far as he knows, that's all his parents think he does. He's chosen not to tell them of his work with Homeland Security."

Rachel felt a spark of hope. If he was using a front like that, maybe Dawson was using the Rileys in his investigation. Maybe his relationship with Vanessa wasn't real. But Kelsey's next words threatened to strangle all hope.

"I have some other guys tracing down some last few details, but from what I see now, John and Vanessa Riley check out too. John Riley is a very successful, very wealthy businessman. His business includes a lot of investing as well as dealing with consumer goods. Dawson and Vanessa attended college together. A few weeks ago, their engagement was announced in the newspaper as well as on Vanessa's Facebook page."

"But there's got to be some reason for Dawson's bizarre behavior," Rachel objected. "Why would he be having a relationship with both Vanessa and me?"

"Lots of guys have multiple girlfriends and secret lives that nobody else knows about," Matthews said with a sneer. "Think about all the celebrities who cheat. Dawson had you, but he also had beautiful, rich, successful Vanessa. Maybe he even had a few more in other cities around the country. The most obvious answer is that he's a two-timing..."

"And thank you, Garrett!" Kelsey interrupted. "If you can survive without Rachel's lovely company for a couple minutes, I still need to take and get her outfitted with all her gear."

Rachel followed Kelsey to a small enclosed room.

"Here is your gun. It's a 40 caliber Glock exactly like Dawson and I carry. You also have one of our special phones and a watch. Both have a special location device so essentially you can be tracked at all times. They do this for your safety as well as just to monitor agents' actions. You are required to have these with you at all times. If your location signal stops moving for a period of time, you will be contacted or agents sent to find you. When you join a government agency like Homeland Security, you give up a lot of your privacy and have to consent to having someone always looking over your shoulder."

"Wait a minute. If Dawson had a watch and cell phone with a tracking device, shouldn't we be able to locate him?"

"Unfortunately, that's the first thing we tried. We found both the phone and the watch, but no Dawson. They had been thrown in a dumpster here in Miami. Added to that, Dawson is unusually good at keeping his privacy. As you know, normally we would know exactly where an agent was and what he was working on when he went missing. Not so with Dawson. Nobody here at the department even knew of his involvement with Vanessa Riley or her father."

Rachel was silent, thinking. Finally, she spoke quietly. "I just don't understand, Kelsey. Why would he get involved with me at the same time as he renewed his relationship with her? It's just seeming more and more like the Dawson Tate I thought I knew doesn't even exist."

"You don't know the whole story, Rachel," Kelsey replied. "Maybe he was working some kind of angle. Maybe Vanessa or her father was some kind of asset that he needed for his investigation. We simply won't know until we talk to him."

"Or maybe I was some kind of asset to him," Rachel said miserably. "Remember that list I gave to Andrews, the one I found in Dawson's Bible? It was a list Dawson had kept of everything I liked and disliked. He even wrote down gift ideas for me. I thought it was so sweet and romantic. But now it looks like he probably needed to write all that stuff down to keep track of which girlfriend liked what!"

Kelsey looked unconvinced. "Come on, Rachel. I really don't think…"

Rachel cut her off. "He's known Vanessa for so long it makes more sense that I am the fake girlfriend! Did you look at her, Kelsey? She's stunning! And she's rich! How can I even compare?"

"I did see her, Rachel. But I've also seen how Dawson looks at you."

"No matter where the truth is, I still have to come to the realization that Dawson is an incredible actor. He's lied to either Vanessa or me." Rachel swallowed and felt tears burning behind her eyes.

She whispered, "And I have this horrible feeling that it's me."

She couldn't look at Kelsey. She knew she would completely fall apart if she did. "It's as if the man I love was just a figment of my imagination, a mirage."

"I know it's hard right now, Rachel," Kelsey said softly. "I know how it looks, and I don't have any answers for you. If you want, I can talk to Andrews about maybe taking you off the case. I understand, and I'm sure he will too. It's too late for you to back out of your contract, but maybe he can just reassign you to another case."

"No!" Rachel said emphatically. Kelsey's words were like a cold splash of water. The threat of tears vanished. There was no way she was going to give up this case, no matter how much it hurt. "Dawson is going to have to look me in the eye and explain himself. I will find him! I will find him even if it's only to kill the man myself!

Chapter 6

With her gun, watch, and cell phone now firmly attached to her person, Rachel returned to Matthews. Kelsey left to continue her own research into the Rileys.

"I have all the information from Dawson's tracking signal," Matthews announced as she approached. "It might be worth tracing the steps he took from the time he landed in Miami. At least we might be able to follow his route until he was abducted and his phone and watch confiscated. It might give us some clues to know exactly where he disappeared. We don't have much else to work with at this point."

"That sounds like a good idea," Rachel said. "Or at least better than anything else we have right now."

Rachel's cell phone rang. It was her old phone, her personal one. Picking it up, she looked at the number and grimaced. "Can you give me a minute,

Matthews? I need to take this call, and then we can leave right away if you want."

Not waiting for a response, not really caring if Matthews consented or not, Rachel answered her phone.

"Hi, Phillip," Rachel answered. "Thanks for calling me back."

Talking to her brother was never the most enjoyable of experiences, and she usually avoided it except for special occasions or emergencies. She was going to try to make this call as quick and painless as possible. "I had an emergency and had to fly to Florida unexpectedly."

"Well, I can't pick you up. You can't stay with me either. I'm not even in Florida right now; I'm in L.A. I wish you'd check with me before you made outrageous plans."

That was her brother, Phillip. As pleasant as ever.

Matthews was obviously listening and watching her with way too much interest. Rachel walked away from the desk, trying to find some privacy in the busy room. Locating what looked like a break room along the perimeter, Rachel hurried inside. Luckily, it was empty at the moment."

"I don't need you to pick me up," she said, trying not to snap. She really didn't need to get into a fight with Philip right now. "I've already made other arrangements. And I certainly didn't expect to stay with you. That's not why I called. You're still flying to Helena tomorrow to see Mom and Dad, right?"

"Yes," he said, his tone wary. "But I'm not staying long this time."

He never stayed long. Truthfully, Rachel didn't know why Phillip even bothered to make regular visits.

Rachel's parents had understood early on that Phillip had his own interests. They had supported and encouraged him in every way, even when they didn't understand him. Because of their unwavering support and financial funding, Phillip had earned a Master's degree in Business and started his own now-thriving company. With all her parents' efforts and all his success, they should have had a close, healthy relationship. But lately, Rachel had been noticing an increased tension, especially between Dad and Phillip.

Now, nobody seemed to enjoy Phillip's visits, least of all him. He always acted uncomfortable and miserable, while her parents tried to cater to him and make him feel welcome. She wondered if Phillip even realized how strained and stressed their parents were when he was around. Rachel herself had a hard time with her older brother because she felt he was selfish and inconsiderate. She didn't like the way he treated their parents and regularly had to bite her tongue, for their sake, to keep from lashing out at him. But despite everything, every month or two, Phillip religiously made a short trip to the ranch, blessing everyone on what appeared to be a very unpleasant chore for him.

Rachel looked up to see Matthews enter the break room. He casually leaned against the counter by the refrigerator and smiled innocently at Rachel. The jerk! He was purposely trying to eavesdrop on her conversation!

Rachel purposely turned her back on Matthews.

"Could you please help Dad with the feedings and any other problems that come up with the ranch?" She asked Phillip outright. She needed to get this conversation over as quickly as possible.

"I don't know, Rachel. I have purposely not done any of that sort of thing since dad made me do it as a teenager. I'm sure he can handle it himself."

"No, Phillip, he can't," Rachel retorted bluntly. "He hasn't been the same since his heart attack. If you don't help him, Mom will try. And if Mom tries, it'll take him twice as long to do anything because she'll insist on detailed instructions for every little task beforehand. They're your parents too, Phillip. Please, help them, just this once"

"Okay, okay! I'll help with the feeding. But if anything more major needs attention, I'm hiring someone else to get it done."

"That's fine. Thank you." Phillip had so much money that she wouldn't care at all if he had to hire someone out of his own wallet. Besides, he was listed as an equal inheritor with her in the ranch. It was high time he started contributing in some way.

"In fact," he continued. "Maybe I should just hire someone to do the feeding too."

"I don't care how it gets done. Do it however you want. Just don't let Dad do it himself."

"Fine, Rachel, but like I said, I'm only staying two or three days. You're emergency trip better be a short one."

"I'm not planning on it being long." She didn't want to even think about what she'd have to do and tell her family when this case was over. She'd have to deal with other arrangements for the ranch later. She could only handle one thing at a time. "Oh, gotta go. Thank you very much for taking care of things, Phillip. I really appreciate it."

Rachel disconnected the call before Phillip could come up with a sarcastic reply to make her feel guilty for even requesting his assistance.

Turning around, she found Matthews still watching her as he munched on a bag of potato chips.

"Okay, Matthews," Rachel said with an exasperated sigh. "What is it that you want?"

"You didn't tell him about joining Homeland Security," he said.

Now he was commenting on her personal phone call? "No, I didn't. Why does it matter to you? It's not like it's any of your business."

Matthews shrugged. "Just curious. You also didn't tell him about Dawson being missing."

"Look, Matthews, my brother and I aren't close. He didn't need to know those things. I need his help until we can find Dawson. Then I'll tell my family about Homeland Security and make other arrangements. Does that meet your approval?"

"Don't call me Matthews," he said making a face. "Call me Garrett, and I'll call you Rachel. I rather detest the way that Andrews calls agents by their first names when they're alone, but refers to them by their last name when anyone else is present. If we're going to be partners, we should be on a first name basis. Call me Garrett."

"Fine," Rachel said.

She needed some coffee. Seeing a pot on the counter, she found a Styrofoam cup and poured it about half full. Then she began adding sugar and creamer. She hated coffee. But she had been awake for well over twenty-four hours, and it didn't look like she was going to be getting sleep anytime soon. She was going to need something to help her stay awake and alert.

"So you're still determined to find Dawson even though he's obviously been lying and cheating on you," Garrett observed.

"Yes, I am. But I still don't think we have the whole story. I think it's still possible that he was involved with Vanessa Riley because he needed her for the case he was working."

Rachel took a sip of the coffee. Nasty. Even with half sugar and cream. She made herself chug it down quickly, as if she was taking foul-tasting medicine

"Were you sleeping with him?"

Completely startled, Rachel almost spewed the coffee. Gagging, she managed to swallow. Coughing, she answered the question before she could even process Garrett's audacity in asking it.

"N-no." She felt herself blushing bright red.

"Have you met his parents?"

"No." Rachel didn't even know why she was answering these invasive questions!

"Has Dawson ever told you he loved you?"

"No, he hasn't." Finally able to catch her breath, Rachel straightened and challenged Garrett with her eyes. What exactly was he getting at?

"Okay, Rachel, let me get this straight. You're not living together, not sleeping together, you've never met his parents, and he's never told you he loved you?"

"Correct." She knew where he was going. And she didn't have a defense.

"So, tell me, Rachel, what exactly is your relationship with Dawson Tate? What makes you even think that you're romantically involved with him, let alone that your relationship is the real one while the one with his fiancé is not? Because, just looking at the facts, you have no relationship."

Garrett was right. Nothing about her relationship with Dawson made sense on paper. Kelsey understood. But how could she explain anything about it to Garrett?

"I know it looks bad," Rachel admitted. "All I can tell you is what I've experienced and what Dawson has told me. As far as I knew, Dawson and I were both Christians. We wanted to wait until marriage for intimacy. I have no explanation for why he never introduced me to his parents or told me he loved me. At least, I didn't until I met Vanessa Riley."

"I'd heard Dawson was a Christian as well," Garret said, his tone softening a little. "I just find that hard to believe when looking at his behavior."

"I'm confused about it right now too. I know this job requires some amount of deception, and I guess I'm still hoping that he has some explanation."

"I'm sorry, Rachel. This job does require deception. In fact, I have to lie on a regular basis in order to investigate my cases and protect the people of this country. However, I can't imagine lying to someone I cared about in the way that Dawson has lied to you. No matter how you look at it, Dawson has completely deceived either you or Vanessa Riley. Even if you are the one he really cares about, are you truly okay with him deceiving Vanessa like he has? I've had to use assets before in ways that I'm not proud, but I have never proposed to a woman and let her plan a wedding, especially knowing I never had the intention of loving her and following through. Part of being a good agent is managing your assets. If Vanessa is just being used, I've never seen an agent handle an asset so poorly and get in so deep."

Garrett was right, Rachel thought miserably. Even if Dawson had been using Vanessa in his case, she would not be okay with a man who treated a woman like he had. He'd proposed to her. She didn't think she could ever get over that he had actually proposed to another woman, no matter what the underlying reason. How could she ever trust him again? Vanessa had seemed nice, had seemed to genuinely love Dawson. Even if they found Dawson and somehow worked things out, how could she love him or continue a relationship knowing he had methodically and deliberately broken Vanessa's heart.

"You know, I used to be a Christian," Garrett mused. But I found that I couldn't be an agent and hold strongly to my convictions. There was too much guilt over the things I had to do. I guess I couldn't do my job if God was involved."

"That's rather ironic," Rachel mused. "I know what this job requires. Though I don't yet have experience, I can imagine the difficult things I'll have to do. I can't speak for Dawson, but for me, I can't imagine doing what I need to do and not having God involved."

Garrett met Rachel's eyes and held her steady gaze. Rachel saw something flicker in their depths, but wasn't sure what it was.

Finally, he spoke, "Well, if Dawson is a shining example of an agent with Christianity, I think I'll pass." A wicked gleam of humor lit his eyes. "I wonder if Dawson shared the same

'Christian convictions' with Vanessa Riley. Somehow she didn't strike me as the type of person who would want to wait until marriage for intimacy."

A chill raced through Rachel and the coffee she had ingested churned in her stomach. Had Dawson been sleeping with Vanessa? Had his Christianity merely been for Rachel's benefit?

Rachel returned Garrett's amused gaze, refusing to let him see her flinch. She may not have all the answers, but she did know two things: One, he unfortunately had a point about Vanessa. And two, she might very well hate Garrett Matthews.

Rachel heard a beep. She looked at the cell phone still clutched in her hand. She had a text message.

"What is it?" Garrett asked. He must have seen the look of shock on Rachel's face. He quickly crossed the room to look over her shoulder.

Rachel whispered hoarsely, "It's from Dawson!"

Chapter 7

Rachel peered at her cell phone screen. "Text message from Dawson Tate sent from his phone 8:10 on Wednesday night! That was the day before yesterday, when Dawson disappeared!"

"And you're just now receiving the message?" Garrett asked, incredulous.

Ignoring him for the moment, Rachel pressed a button and read aloud, "3252 Fairmont. Miami."

"It's an address!" Garrett exclaimed. Quickly, he turned and literally ran out of the break room and back to his desk. Rachel followed.

As he typed the address into the computer, Rachel tried to explain. "Either my cell phone or my provider stinks! We don't have many choices for service in the area of Montana where I live. I frequently don't receive messages when they're actually sent. Two days late is fairly typical."

"If we had gotten this address when we should have…" Garrett didn't finish his sentence.

Rachel felt sick to her stomach. She knew it wasn't her fault, but she still felt responsible. What if it was too late now? What if Dawson had been killed? What if they could have prevented it if she had only received the text on time?

"It's a bank," Garrett announced, looking at a map on the computer screen. Quickly, he grabbed several strange looking items off his desk and stuffed them in a bag. "Let's go."

Rachel hurried to follow as Garrett ran for the elevator.

Twenty minutes later, they were parking outside a large bank. Both Rachel and Garrett had been completely silent on the drive.

Turning off the car, Garrett turned and finally spoke. "Look, Rachel. Don't torture yourself about the text message. There's nothing you could have done. We just need to work with what we have now. Do you have any idea why Dawson would send you the address of this bank?"

"No, I don't. He's never mentioned it before."

"Let's think about this. If Dawson knew he was in danger, he would send someone a clue to help them know what he was doing or help them find him."

Rachel nodded. "Andrews said Dawson claimed he always had a failsafe–a backup for all of his investigations should something unexpected happen to him. Andrews thought I was the failsafe."

"So, obviously Dawson sent you this address, intending for you to come here. Maybe there's something here he wanted you to find."

Rachel wracked her brain. Money? Could Dawson have an account here? No. It probably had something to do with his case. He'd want to make sure his files were in the right hands should something happen to him.

Suddenly, she had an idea. Quickly rummaging through her bag, she located the set of keys Dawson had given her. There were about ten keys on the ring, varying in size from small to the large one that unlocked his gun cabinet.

"What about a safety deposit box, Garrett?" she asked. "Banks have those, right? What if Garrett has a safety deposit box with all his case files? He would have had to previously give me the key. Then when he had to, he would just send me the address of the bank."

"That's brilliant, Rachel! You have his keys?"

"Yes," she said, holding up the ring to show him. "Dawson gave these all to me months ago in case I ever needed to open something of his when he was gone."

"Okay, here's how we have to play this thing," Garret said, speaking quickly. "We won't get anywhere if we go in and make demands as government agents. They insist on the proper warrants and other verifications, which we really don't have time to get. You're going to have to go in alone. If Dawson has a safety deposit box in there that he intended you to access, then he will have taken measures to make sure you could do so."

Garrett rummaged around in the sack he'd carried out of the office. Taking out a small earpiece, he handed it to Rachel. "Put this in your ear. I will be able to talk to you if needed. Attach this other small wire somewhere inside your shirt. Now I'll be able to hear what you hear. You'd better leave your gun here. You can't go in there as an agent. Obviously, I can't go inside with you. Dawson would have intended you to go alone."

"Okay, here I go," Rachel said, removing her Glock and leaving it on the floor of the car. She could tell that Garrett didn't want to waste any time, and she didn't either. They finally had a lead, and she didn't want to give herself the chance to think about the task in front of her. She had no idea what she was going to do or say once she got inside, but she put one foot in front of the other and entered Regent Bank.

As she walked across the tiled floor to the counter, she heard Garrett speak.

"Think, Rachel, think! What are you going to say? Dawson probably wouldn't use your real name, but something you would readily know or be able to figure out."

"May I help you?" the middle aged, balding man behind the counter asked with a friendly smile.

Rachel returned his smile and started speaking before she even knew what she was going to say. "Yes, I have a safety deposit box, but honestly, I'm not sure what the number is since I'm not the one who usually accesses it."

"That won't be a problem as long as we have you on file," the man assured. "I can just look up the account. What is your name?"

Here it was. What was her name? What name would Dawson use?

"Montana," Rachel blurted. Dawson would think it absolutely hilarious to use his nickname for her. The more she thought about it, the more sure she was.

The man typed on the computer. She waited. This had to work. She had no other options.

"And there you are!" he announced. "Mrs. Holly Montana?"

"Yes, that's me," Rachel replied. Such relief!

"Now do you have a key to the box?"

"Yes, I do, but I'm not sure which one it is," she held up her key ring.

"Oh, that's not a problem, Mrs. Montana. I'll go back to the vault with you and assist you with opening it. I don't even need to see your photo ID as your husband provided it when he opened the account, and we have your picture saved here on the computer. I can see you are definitely Mrs. Holly Montana. I just need you to sign here for our records that you accessed the box, and then I can take you back."

Rachel signed quickly, then paused.

"Do you think you could tell me when my *husband* last accessed the box? He was recently supposed to put some important papers inside, but I'm not sure if he ever got it done."

"Oh, certainly. Just let me look it up. Let's see. Woodrow Montana accessed his safety deposit box on Wednesday. Oh, that's right! I remember. I was the one who assisted him. Wood came in right before we closed. He was in a big hurry. Probably worried he wouldn't make it in time to put in those papers you wanted him to."

"Good!" Rachel said. "That definitely makes me feel better knowing he got it done. He's been so busy lately I wasn't sure."

"Now, if you'll follow me, Mrs. Montana. I'll take you to your box."

"Rachel, you're doing absolutely fantastic!" she heard Garrett speaking in her ear.

When they reached the vault, Rachel handed the man her keys. He quickly sorted through them and separated out a small silver one. He inserted it into the silver box number 239. Sliding it out, he handed Rachel back her keys and carried the box back outside to a viewing room.

"I'll leave you here with your box, Mrs. Montana. Take as much time as you need."

"Thank you."

Wasting no time, Rachel opened the box. There was a yellow manila envelope inside. Opening it, she found a thick sheaf of papers. She pulled them out halfway and knew immediately what they were. Dawson's case file. Flipping through, she saw everything from building schematics to both handwritten and typed notes. Rachel's hands shook. This is what they needed. With this information, they would surely be able to locate Dawson.

Garrett's voice remained quiet, apparently content to let her focus on getting the job done and wait for his update after she was in the clear.

Sliding the papers back into the envelope, she went to put the lid back on the empty box and stopped. There was one item still in it. It was a gun. A Walther 9 mm. Attached to the gun was a yellow sticky note with one word, 'Montana.' It was a small gun, much smaller and thinner than the department-issued Glock. It was the exact kind Rachel had taken off a terrorist in New York. She had, of course, had to surrender it as evidence in the investigation, but Dawson had known how much she liked it.

Rachel quickly stuck the gun in her bag, reassembled the box, and took it back to the vault. Holding the envelope tightly, she quickly walked back to the lobby and started for the front doors.

"Mrs. Montana! Wait!"

It was the voice of the man who had helped her. Maybe he had somehow found out that about the fake name. Maybe her signature didn't match the one they had on file. Should she stop or make a run for it?

Rachel stopped and turned with a smile on her face. She would draw more attention if she ran than if she acted as if nothing was wrong.

"Steady, Rachel, steady." the voice in her ear urged.

"I'm glad I caught you! The other day your husband left so quickly that I wasn't able to give him this information." The man handed her several papers stapled together. "We have many new options for accounts, banking, savings, CDs, IRAs. We would be very appreciative if you and your husband would consider us for your other banking needs."

"Thank you," Rachel replied. "I'll be sure my husband takes a look at it."

And she fully intended that Dawson would take a look at the papers. As she walked out the bank doors, the option she liked best was taping them to his toilet seat. Maybe then he would understand just how much she *appreciated* his method of making her his failsafe. Why did he make her jump through all these hoops when he could have just told her or given her the info?

"What do we have?" Garrett asked as Rachel slid into the front seat.

"A Walther 9 mm with my name on it, literally. And... Dawson's case file," Rachel announced, waving the envelope.

"That should help," Garrett said. "Let's head back to the office and take a look. You were brilliant in there, by the way. How did you know Dawson put the account under the name Montana?"

"Montana is the nickname Dawson gave me the first day we met. He really started doing it to taunt me and then it just stuck." Rachel didn't mention that nowadays Dawson used her nickname more as an endearment. "When I was in there trying to figure out what name to give, it suddenly occurred to me that Dawson would have thought it hilarious to put the account under the name Montana. I knew without a doubt that he would have used my nickname and thought himself extremely clever for doing so."

Rachel laughed in spite of herself. "The jerk probably thought himself even more clever for calling us 'Woodward and Holly Montana.' When he started calling me Montana, I dubbed him 'Hollywood,' saying the name 'Dawson Tate' sounded more like a fake, stage name."

But nowadays, unlike Dawson, Rachel couldn't say she used his nickname for endearment. Instead, she still used it to tease and taunt him whenever necessary.

"At least you got the file," Garrett said.

"Yeah, but what if I hadn't? Seems stupid to create all these obstacles when he could have just told me or left simple instructions."

Garrett shrugged. "He had reasons that made sense to him. Besides, easy and straightforward is not Dawson's style. At least he knew you well enough that he was sure you'd figure out how to get access to that box."

"Still seems stupid, if you ask me. But none of Dawson's decisions lately are making sense to me."

As Garrett drove, Rachel looked through Dawson's file, reporting to Garrett the snippets that she understood from a quick survey.

By the time they arrived back at their temporary office, Garrett and Rachel knew that their suspicions had been correct. Dawson had been investigating John Riley in connection with the terrorist ring and attempted bombing in New York.

In spite of herself, Rachel was elated. "So this means Dawson was just using Vanessa Riley in his investigation, right?

She, Kelsey, and Dawson were all gathered around the desk in a room with a large conference table, spreading out and passing around the papers in Dawson's file.

"Not necessarily," Kelsey said. "I'm reading some of Dawson's notes right now that state very emphatically that he has found not even a hint of evidence that connects Vanessa Riley to this case in any way, just her father. It is very likely that Dawson did use their relationship to try to gain information, but there is no telling what his actual feelings are about it. Remember, they've known each other long before Dawson was assigned this case. And also remember that they are engaged, which seems unnecessary and unwise if he just viewed her as an asset."

Why did she keep getting her hopes up? Rachel thought, feeling rather angry with herself. Right now, it was very unlikely that she'd want Dawson back at all, even if Vanessa turned out to be just an asset.

Andrews had been right. Dawson kept meticulous notes and his case file was very thorough. Everything he did in connection to the case, every lead, even every suspicion was documented.

"He has no evidence," Garrett announced, reaching the end of the file and handing the last page to Kelsey. "All he has is his suspicions, and, yes, some good circumstantial evidence like these pictures of some of Riley's employees meeting with suspected terrorists. But he has no hard evidence, especially on John Riley himself."

"But look at his last notes," Kelsey said, pointing to the last entries on the page she was holding. "Dawson had found a source–someone who claimed to have evidence proving John Riley's involvement. Dawson was arranging to meet with him before he disappeared."

Garrett rubbed his hand over his face tiredly. "The only explanation that makes sense is that John Riley found out what Dawson was doing and either abducted him or had him killed. Unfortunately, we have no idea where he would have taken him. We also have no evidence. We don't even have enough for a search warrant. And it would be pointless to bring him in for questioning. We have nothing."

"Maybe not," Rachel said, looking at the paper in front of her. "These are the building specs on John Riley's house. There are also two floor plans of this same house. Look at them side by side. You see the difference?"

"The basement!" Garrett said.

"Exactly! Dawson circled these rooms on this plan. They don't even exist on the other one. They must be some kind of secret rooms. If Riley kept Dawson alive, there might be a good chance he's hiding him there."

"Sounds like a long shot," Kelsey said. "Besides, there's no way we could gain access to those rooms. Like Garrett said, we don't even have enough evidence for a search warrant."

"What if we snuck in?" Rachel asked with a smile.

"You mean like breaking and entering?" Garrett asked. "Rachel, that house probably has security to rival Fort Knox."

"It wouldn't be breaking and entering if we were already at the house as invited guests," Rachel said. "Didn't Vanessa say their engagement party was tonight? She did say she would do *anything* to help us with the investigation. I'm sure she'd give us an invitation if we said we needed to observe some of her other guests. Then we can just sneak down to the basement area when no one is watching and see what we find."

Garrett's grin was wide by the time Rachel finished talking. "Well, Rachel, it sounds like you have a plan. How about we go crash a party?"

Chapter 8

Rachel slid the tight-fitting dress over her head and wiggled into it.

Her cell phone rang on the counter. Picking it up, she recognized the number.

"Hi, Dad," she answered, cradling the phone against her shoulder as she adjusted the dress against her hips.

"Hi, Sweetheart. I'm calling for an update."

"There's not much to tell yet, Dad. We have a lead, but we aren't sure anything will come of it."

"Come on, Rachel. You said Dawson was in trouble. I'm going to need a little more than that."

Rachel sighed. She was going to have to think of something to tell her dad.

She zipped up the hidden zipper on the side, and the dress clung to her form even more. Now, where to put her gun? The Glock obviously wasn't going to work. Seeing a small strappy thing near the heels Kelsey had given her, Rachel quickly began strapping her Walther 9 mm to her upper calf.

"Dad, you know Dawson works for Homeland Security. I really can't tell you more than that. I already explained when you wanted to come to Florida with me. Dawson's case is highly classified."

"Then how is it that you know about it?"

Great, she'd walked right into that one.

Choosing her words carefully, she answered her dad, "I found a way so they would let me in on the investigation."

"Rachel..." her dad practically growled as if he had a bad feeling about what she had done."

She was going to have to change the subject. Fast.

"Don't worry, Dad. Everything is fine." She worked to keep all tension out of her voice, trying to pretend that she wasn't really strapping a gun to her leg in preparation of essentially breaking into the house of a suspected domestic terrorist. "I'll fill you in as soon as I find out something. Now, I talked to Phillip, and he said he'd help out with the feeding when he arrives tomorrow."

Rachel let the skirt on her dress fall and examined her work. The gun was so thin, it sat close to her leg and wasn't visible under the material. It was on the opposite side of the long slit, so it shouldn't even show when she walked.

"Rachel, I'm not sure I need Phillip's kind of help."

"You can't do it all yourself, Dad. Besides, I have a feeling Phillip will wimp out and just hire someone to help anyway. I really have to go, now, Dad. We're getting ready to follow up on that lead. I'll call you later, okay."

"You'd better. If I don't hear from you in the next twenty-four hours, I'm going to fly down to Florida no matter what you say."

When she'd left Montana, she had tried to stick with the basic truth, telling her parents that Dawson was in trouble, so she had to fly down to Florida to help. Her dad had immediately started gathering his things to go with her. It had been hard enough to convince him not to come. He had finally relented for the time being, settling on driving Rachel to the airport and making her promise to call as soon as she knew anything.

Signing off, she sighed, trying to release all the stress of her dad's call. Finally, she looked at herself in the bathroom mirror. Couldn't Kelsey have gotten her an evening dress made with a little more material?

Honestly, Rachel knew there was nothing immodest about the dress. It was a simple black gown with a v-neck, open back, and long slitted skirt. Rachel just felt awkward. The last time she wore evening attire had probably been her high school prom, and that dress had definitely had better coverage, at her dad's insistence.

She knew she really had no reason to feel so awkward. The dress looked good on her; she was slender and it hugged her in all the right places. And, it definitely wasn't as bad as that hooker outfit Dawson had made her wear when they were trying to escape the terrorists in New York.

Quickly she twisted her hair up into what she imagined might resemble a sophisticated style in the right lighting. Sticking a few more bobby pins in her hair for good measure, she took a deep breath, and left the bathroom.

"Rachel, you look great!" Kelsey said when she entered the small room they had confiscated for planning.

Garrett was there as well, looking like a movie star decked out in an elegant black tux.

Rachel saw Garrett looking her over, but he said nothing. She should have just been satisfied that he didn't make some sarcastic comment, but she couldn't resist just one little jab.

"That's okay, Garrett. You don't have to say anything nice. I know it doesn't come naturally to you. You do clean up decently well yourself." Not waiting for his response, she turned to Kelsey. "Thanks for coming up with all this on such short notice."

"No problem. I'm glad everything worked."

"I don't have any room for my Glock, though," Rachel said, handing the weapon to Kelsey. "I guess you'll have to babysit it for me. I managed to get the Walther on my person, but this dress doesn't exactly have pockets to store equipment."

"That's fine," Garrett said. "We aren't authorized to use any kind of deadly force on this mission anyway. We have to go in without any weapons at all. Go ahead and keep your Walther though. I think it would be unwise to go in completely unarmed. Besides, what Andrews doesn't know won't hurt him."

At Rachel's look of confusion, Kelsey spoke up. "Strictly speaking, this isn't a department-sanctioned mission."

"What do you mean?" Rachel asked with a sense of foreboding.

Garrett took up the explanation. "Andrews wants us to go to the party and snoop around the basement, but it'll be a mission off the record. We can't go in there as Homeland Security agents. That means deadly force is not an option, and we won't have backup. We're on our own."

"But why?" Rachel asked, not liking the sound of this mission.

"John Riley is an important man," Kelsey said. "He's rich and influential, with plenty of political connections and friends in high places. We have no evidence. We have no warrant. We only have Dawson's suspicions and now our own. Andrews cannot authorize such a potentially risky mission. If this goes south and Homeland Security is implicated, it would be disastrous for the department."

Rachel closed her eyes. "So the end result is that we are tasked with breaking and entering a high-security mansion blind with no weapons and no backup. Oh, and we can't get caught."

"Well, you won't quite be blind and without backup," Kelsey said. "I'll be outside in a van and hopefully tapped into the mansion's security control panel."

"Can you do that?" Rachel asked.

"Yes, she can," Garrett replied. "I think Andrews won't let Kelsey be a lead field agent because she is the best he has at working behind the scenes. It also helps that she is a pretty wicked hacker."

"I try," Kelsey said with a smile.

Before Rachel could fully analyze and appreciate the seemingly impossible task before them, she was walking into the luxurious Riley mansion on Garrett's arm. Kelsey was already in position and parked in a van outside. Though she wouldn't be coming into the house, she was attending as the voice in each of their ears. The earpieces Kelsey had given Garrett and Rachel had been so tiny and clear that they were almost invisible when in the ear.

Vanessa Riley immediately greeted them as they entered the door. It had been relatively easy to call her and obtain an invitation to the party. She'd seemed a little unnerved by the idea that one of her guests might be involved in Dawson's disappearance, but she was eager to do anything to help them with the investigation. She'd even offered to let Rachel borrow one of her dresses if she needed it for the party.

"Please let me know if you need anything," Vanessa said, taking each of their hands in a warm squeeze. "My dad already let his security team know of the situation, so they're here to assist in whatever you may need. I just hope you're able to find some kind of lead on Dawson. I'm not sure how much more of this I can take! And now, having to pretend that everything is fine..."

Vanessa's eyes teared, and she struggled to regain control.

"We're certainly doing all we can to find him," Garrett said sympathetically.

Rachel spoke up. "Just so you know, Miss Riley. We may not be staying long. Whether or not we find what we need, we'll probably have to slip away quickly to follow any leads or work other angles."

Vanessa nodded her understanding, and then moved to greet some other guests while Rachel and Garrett found the ballroom.

"So much for the plan," Garrett gritted out.

"I guess when we said to tell absolutely no one of our presence or purpose here, she didn't think that 'no one' included her father."

"Or his whole security team," Garrett added.

"Just get in and start assessing the situation," came Kelsey's voice in their ears. "If we need to adapt the plan, we will once we figure out what we're up against."

They walked around the perimeter of the crowded room, finally ending at the food. The party was already in full swing, with couples dancing in the middle, crowded in groups along the side, and eating elaborate delicacies. Rachel's nerves were strung tight. There were so many people, and she had no idea what she and Garrett were supposed to be looking for. Garrett, on the other hand, appeared very relaxed and began helping himself to some of the hor d'oeuvres.

"Want some?" Garrett offered, gesturing to his plate of shrimp.

"No thanks," Rachel replied, her eyes scanning the room. The thought of food made her stomach turn.

"Come on, Rachel. It's part of the job. We can learn a lot about who we are up against simply by sampling the appetizers."

Rachel sent him a look that said she thought he was being absolutely ridiculous.

"For instance," Garrett explained, "by tasting the Rileys' food, I can tell they are extremely rich, very focused on appearances, and careful about even the smallest details. That can be a formidable combination."

"So you're saying the food is good," Rachel summarized with a roll of her eyes.

"Delicious," Garrett said with appreciation.

"Look, Garrett," Rachel said with obvious frustration. "Can we just get on with it? I'm really not interested in the Rileys' delicious food or their exceptional taste. I am interested in doing what we came here to do."

"Fine," he said, wiping his mouth with a napkin and setting down his empty plate. "Shall we dance then?"

Without waiting for Rachel's reply, he grabbed her elbow and pulled her out to the middle of the dance floor. Holding her close, he immediately started moving to the music.

"Uh, Garrett," Rachel said, caught off-guard by the sudden change in activity. "I don't really dance."

Rachel felt her face turning pink. "Or perhaps I should say, I don't know how to dance. At all."

Garrett looked at her with a smile, as if he finally had the advantage.

"No problem. Consider this lesson one. Dancing is a great skill to have as an agent. Just stay real close and follow my lead."

Garrett held her so close she could smell his spicy cologne. His proximity made her very uncomfortable and yet she also had the strange urge to simply relax into his strong arms. Her mind fought both sensations, and it was challenging to give up control and let Garrett take the lead. The longer she did it, though, the easier it became as Garrett whisked her completely around the room.

Kelsey's voice sounded in Rachel's ear. "I'm going to have to sign off for a few minutes while I go make some adjustments to the equipment. Sit tight. I'll be back in a few."

Rachel was becoming increasingly impatient. Were they never going to make their move? Dawson could be locked in the basement at this very minute, and they were dancing?

"Garrett, what exactly are we doing?" She couldn't take it anymore. "Shouldn't we be focusing on our mission?"

Garrett looked at her in surprise. "I am. With this short dance around the room, I can gain a perspective on everyone here. Specifically, I'm identifying the security. Since they are already aware of our presence, we need to be aware of theirs. Besides, I'm rather enjoying dancing with the most beautiful woman in the room."

Rachel looked at him sharply. Was he being sarcastic again? But, no, he was looking at her steadily with not even a glint of humor in his gray eyes.

Holding her even closer, he whispered in her ear. "In fact, I should probably warn you. If you don't stop being so beautiful and incredible in all you do, I may make it my mission to sweep you off your feet and make you forget Dawson Tate ever existed."

Rachel pulled back in confusion and looked at his face. Was he serious? His eyes beckoned, pulling her like magnets. And yet she suddenly felt vulnerable. His warm hand against her bare back sent goosebumps over her entire body. What was happening?

Recent events with Dawson had made her feel both deceived and undesirable, like there must be something wrong with her. Now Garrett was looking at her like he wanted to pull her into his arms and never let her go. Could she trust him? Did she even want to?

"Okay, I'm back," Kelsey said into the earpiece.

The moment, or whatever it had been, was broken.

"And it's not good news." Kelsey continued. "From everything I see Riley's security thinks you two are the main attraction tonight. Their eyes are on you wherever you moved. When you went to the food table, about ten different men readjusted their positions. Your dancing around the room has them scrambling."

"That's pretty much what I've observed too," Garrett said. "There's no way we're going to be able to slip downstairs and go unnoticed."

"So what do we do?" Rachel asked.

Garrett grimaced. "We'll have to go with a modified version of your first idea, Rachel–breaking and entering. Kelsey, you need to get a firm grip on the security system. Rachel and I are going to make our exit."

Garrett guided Rachel back toward the entrance, but he chose a route that took them close to where Vanessa was holding court. Someone was pressing a microphone in her hand, and it looked like she was getting ready to speak to the group. As they passed, Garrett seemed to catch Vanessa's eye, nod, and wave. Vanessa nodded her understanding right before stepping onto a small platform and raising her voice to get everyone's attention.

"Perfect timing," Garrett said quietly. "Vanessa and her security will know we're leaving, but they'll be distracted by Vanessa's speaking."

As they made their way to the front door, Rachel could hear Vanessa thanking everyone for coming and expertly explaining Dawson's absence. Vanessa was completely charming, and Rachel had the feeling that, by the time she was done, her audience would have found it stranger for Dawson to be present at his own engagement party than absent.

When Rachel and Garrett reached the car, he finally explained. "They need to think we left. That way they won't expect us to sneak back inside.

He drove a few blocks, then parked in the shadows. Getting out of the car, they backtracked and started up a long drive that disappeared into some trees.

"What are we doing?" Rachel asked. "Can we actually get into the house through another entrance?"

"I hope so." Garrett replied. "Kelsey, are you tapped into the security?

"Yes, I'm in. And, yes the service entrance is unlocked. Riley has so many employees working this party that there's been plenty of traffic back there."

By the time they walked up to the entrance at the back of the house, Rachel's feet were killing her. She wished Kelsey would have found an alternative to heels. Unfortunately, they weren't very functional for walking long distances and going on secret government missions.

As they approached the door, Kelsey spoke, "I got you covered. Security isn't seeing your approach. This entrance leads directly into a large kitchen, almost like one you would find in a commercial restaurant, not a house. From what I can see on the security feed, everyone is very busy. You might be able to slip in unnoticed.

Wasting no time, Garrett opened the door, and he and Rachel slipped inside. The door shut behind him, emitting a loud, ear-piercing squeak.

Work in the kitchen suddenly stopped, and at least seven pairs of eyes locked onto the intruders.

Chapter 9

So much for being inconspicuous.

Rachel and Garrett froze. Rachel's mind scrambled and grabbed onto the first idea that popped into her head.

"Oh, Sweetheart," Rachel said suddenly, trying to slur her words and make large, unsteady gestures. "Did we get the wrong entrance? No, I'm sure this is the right one. We just went out for some fresh air and came right back in. How did they move the ballroom so fast?"

Catching on, Garrett looked around the room and spoke with an equally slurred British accent. "Would anyone be so kind to direct us to where they moved the ballroom?"

Seven arms almost comically extended and pointed.

"Down the long hall," one white-capped worker said. "Large door on the right."

Thankfully, none of the busy workers seemed to have the inclination to be an escort for the couple who had obviously had a little too much of the free alcohol.

"Thank you," Garrett said cheerfully, leading the way as Rachel walked beside him, adding just the right amount of weave to her slightly unsteady gait.

As they passed into the hallway, Kelsey spoke. "On your left, there's something labeled on the floor plan as an employee supply room."

The hallway was empty and Garrett quickly opened the door and shut and locked it behind them. Thankfully, there was no one else in the room. One wall was filled with lockers. The other side had a long rack with employee uniforms.

"Remind me later to compliment you on your quick thinking back there," Garrett said. But, now, we need to do a quick wardrobe change. We'll get a lot farther if we can blend in with the other employees. Garrett immediately took off his suit jacket and tie and started putting on what looked like a white chef's shirt over his dress shirt. Rachel nervously picked up a pair of baggy pants. How was she going to do this modestly?

"No time to be shy, Rachel," Garrett said, as if reading her mind. "Hurry up and get it done."

"She didn't care what Garrett said, she was not going to disrobe in front of him. She quickly pulled the white shirt over her dress, and then pulled the baggy pants over her long skirt. She rolled up the skirt to her waist, so it wouldn't be so obvious. The only thing that made her nervous was her heels. She had no other shoes to replace them with, so they would have to do. Hopefully, no one would notice. By the time she turned around, Garrett was looking like ridiculously-handsome kitchen help.

Exiting the supply room, they continued down the hall. But, instead of reentering the ballroom, they followed Kelsey's instructions to a small elevator and boarded. Garrett pressed the button to the basement level, and the elevator descended.

"Here we go, Kelsey," he said instead. I certainly hope you're accessing the security feed on this floor as well."

"Of course," Kelsey replied. "But we do need to hurry. I have no idea how long I will remain undetected."

The elevator came to a stop, and the door slid open.

"Thankfully, it's pretty deserted down here," Kelsey reported as she directed them through the maze of what looked like offices. "There are a few people still around though, so this isn't the most direct route."

"Riley probably conducts a lot of his legitimate business from these offices," Garrett observed quietly.

"And saves his more illegal activities for the secret rooms no one knows about?" Rachel asked.

"Let's hope so," Garrett replied.

"Okay, there should be a large office straight ahead," Kelsey said. "From the blueprints in Dawson's file, it looks like the entrance to the secret rooms is in there. I don't have eyes in there, though. There isn't a security camera. You're going in blind."

Garrett soundlessly opened the door a crack. The lights were off and everything was dark. Without hesitation, Garrett opened the door the rest of the way and slipped inside. Rachel followed.

The large office was empty except for equally large furniture. The walls were lined with bookcases on all sides. A massive, rather ostentatious desk sat center in the room. Garrett flipped the light switch, flooding the room with a soft glow.

"This must be Riley's office," Garrett said.

"But there is no door to other rooms," Rachel said.

"It must be hidden somewhere," Kelsey said. "That's definitely the right room."

"Maybe one of these bookcases moves aside somehow," Garrett mused.

"Would Riley really be so cliché?" Rachel asked, beginning to wander around the room.

"Yes, he would," Garrett said firmly. "You're talking about a man who is wrapped in his own importance. One of the hallmarks of an important, untouchable man is the hidden room behind the bookcase."

Garrett methodically began searching through each bookcase. Rachel searched the desk. The top of the desk was clean with only a few pictures and other objects, mainly for the sake of appearance. She made a quick search of the drawers. Nothing.

She went back through each drawer, lifting the contents of each, and inspecting every inch of the interior. Again, nothing.

She stepped back and looked at the desk. If there was a hidden drawer or something, she should be able to see if the frame was larger somewhere than the drawer size. There! The bottom part of the desk looked a little deeper than the drawer had been.

She pulled it out again. But the bottom was solid, not false. Frustrated, she pushed the drawer in hard and jiggled it around. Something clicked, moving the drawer further inside the desk. There was now about a two inch space between the exterior of the desk and the where the drawer was pushed in. Reaching down into the space, she felt a small button. Could it really be that simple? She pushed the button. The bookshelf directly in back of the desk moved aside, revealing a large door.

"Good work, Rachel!" Garrett said, moving quickly toward the door. "Kelsey, there's some kind of security lock on the door. You're going to have to work some magic."

Garrett carefully removed the plastic exterior of a small display and keypad. Removing a small wire attached to a black box resembling a calculator, he plugged the wire into the security box.

"Give me a couple minutes," Kelsey said.

Rachel's nerves felt as tight as violin strings. This was taking too long! She just knew they were going to get caught any minute. She went back, adjusted the desk drawer back to its original position and flipped off the light. It would be better if it appeared they had never been there.

"Open sesame," Kelsey announced, and the hidden door slid open. A dark corridor loomed in front of them.

"Thanks, Kelsey," Garrett said. "I don't suppose you have security access to these rooms."

"No, I don't. For all intent and purposes, these rooms don't exist."

"Great. This should be fun."

They walked into the corridor, and Garrett pressed a button on the wall. They saw the bookcase moving back into place right before the hidden door slid shut. Rachel tried to keep her heels quiet as they walked cautiously down the eerily silent hall. Every time they came to a door, Garrett would open it and look inside. The rooms were just more offices– annoyingly innocent, sterile, non-incriminating offices.

Rachel felt nausea return in waves. It was looking more and more like their theory was wrong. There was no evidence of illegal activity here. If they got caught, they would be in serious trouble on so many levels.

Garrett opened the last door. He paused, then slipped inside. Rachel followed. There were three other doors along one wall. Too many to be just closets. Garrett walked over to the middle door. With a jolt of excitement, she suddenly saw what had caught his eye. There was a security panel to the right of it. There was no handle.

Garrett spoke, "Kelsey, we have a door with a security panel that looks very similar to the other one."

Like before, Garrett removed the plastic cover and inserted the small wire.

After about a minute. Kelsey spoke. "This code isn't the same as the other one. Fortunately, though, we have all the newest technology. It is very hard nowadays to have a completely secure code, especially something secure from the government. Riley really should invest in a fingerprint or retinal scanner. He's behind the times."

"You'll have to suggest it to him next time you see him," Garrett replied sarcastically.

Rachel spoke up, "Well, if what you say about him is true, Garrett, he probably doesn't even think he needs to invest in better security. He sounds overly confident. He probably has underlings do most of his dirty work anyway. It would be too much of a hassle to have a retinal or fingerprint scanner when he needed to send in someone else."

"I guess it doesn't really matter," Kelsey said. "The important thing is that it works in our favor. Got it."

The door opened.

A man sat in the corner of the small, dark room.

He looked up, his eyes colliding with Rachel's. "Dawson!"

Chapter 10

Rachel rushed passed Garret and kneeled next to Dawson. Her eyes strained in the dim light, trying to take inventory of any injuries.

"Rachel, what are you doing here?" Dawson asked, his voice raspy and his eyes blinking as they tried to adjust to the light from the open door now flooding the room.

"Finding you, of course!" Rachel replied.

"We'll have to save the pleasantries for later," Garrett said at Rachel's elbow. "We need to get out of here."

Dawson struggled to stand. Garrett took his hand and helped pull him up.

"Dawson, are you hurt?" Rachel asked, alarmed at his obvious weakness.

"I'll live."

Dawson took two steps toward the door and stumbled. Garrett immediately took a position on Dawson's right side, placing his arm across the back of his shoulders to help support his weight. Rachel did the same on his left side.

"Kelsey, Dawson is injured," Garrett reported. This might take a bit longer than we expected. We're also going to need some kind of plan to get him out of the house without being seen."

"I'm not sure how much longer we have, Garrett. Security is sure to start getting suspicious soon. It's only a matter of time before they figure out they've been hacked."

They made it back through the corridor, but having to support Dawson's weight made it very slow going. Pushing the button on the wall again, the secret door opened, the bookshelf moved, and they made it back through Riley's office. This time, they didn't take the time to close everything and cover their tracks.

As they emerged into the fully lighted office hallway, Rachel gasped. Dawson's face was bruised and bloody. His left eye was dark and swollen and dried blood smeared his face from a cut on his forehead. The darkness of the other rooms had hidden his injuries, and now Rachel saw they were more severe than she had realized. One or both of his legs must also be injured as he was still unable to support his own weight, and Rachel didn't know how she and Garrett could practically carry him out, especially without being seen.

"Garrett, there's no way we can escape like this," Rachel said.

"I know, but obviously Dawson can't walk. How are we going to carry him out without being seen?"

Rachel's eyes focused on a large black garbage can on wheels positioned along the wall. It looked like the janitor had left it there intending to come back later and finish. A crazy idea popped into her head.

"Garrett, let's put him in that garbage can! Then we can just wheel him out like we're taking the trash out!"

"Brilliant, Rachel!" Garrett said, pushing Dawson toward the large cylinder.

It took some maneuvering, but Dawson didn't complain, and they eventually had him in the can and upright. For good measure, they piled a few empty boxes on top of his head, so it looked as if the garbage was definitely full. This time, Kelsey directed them on the most direct route to the elevator. They hurried, the inescapable roar from the wheels of the heavy can echoing through the silent hall. The elevator was in sight. Just a little further.

"Hide! Quick!" Kelsey urged suddenly. "Someone is coming around the corner!"

The corner was in between them and the elevator. There was no time to make a dash for it.

Garrett flung open one of the office doors to the right. He and Rachel pushed the garbage can inside the dark room. Garrett quickly but softly shut the door.

"He heard you!" Kelsey's frantic voice reported. "He's stopping! Get out of sight!"

There was no time and no place to hide!

Garrett suddenly pushed Rachel up against the wall. Before she could form a single word, his lips were on hers, his kiss rough and demanding. What was he thinking? Rachel started to push him away, but abruptly stopped when she suddenly understood what he was doing.

Placing her hands on his chest, she leaned in, eagerly returning his kiss. Garrett groaned slightly and pulled her even closer. His kiss slowed, deepened. His fingers tangled in her hair. His passion was intoxicating, taking Rachel's breath away, making her heart pound, and awakening an insatiable hunger.

The bright light blinked on, blinding them. Startled, they broke apart and turned toward the intruder at the door, surprised and guilty expressions flawlessly pasted on their faces. Rachel felt her face already turning red, and unfortunately, she knew it wasn't entirely an act.

"What are you doing in here?" The man at the door demanded. By the dress shirt and tie, Rachel knew he must be one of Riley's office employees. He was short, bald, and wore both a pair of glasses and an outraged expression on his face.

Garrett answered hesitantly. "Um, we were sent down here to pick up any garbage that needed to be taken out. And I guess we, um… got a little distracted."

The man sneered. "Just get out of here and get back to work before I decide to tell your supervisor about your little distraction."

"Yes, sir, right away," Garrett replied, as both he and Rachel began moving the garbage can back out into the hall.

They finished walking to the elevator, and then stood in excruciating silence as they waited for it to arrive. Finally, a beep announced the elevator's arrival. They hurriedly stepped inside and turned around. As the doors closed, they could see the man still watching them warily from the hallway. He may have let them go, but he was definitely still suspicious. The split second before the doors shut completely, Rachel thought she saw his eyes focus on something. She looked down, following his gaze. Her high-heeled shoes.

The instant the elevator started moving, Dawson popped up in the garbage can and punched Garrett in the jaw.

"Dawson, no!" Rachel gasped.

"Don't you ever touch her again!" he said, the deadly calm of his voice contrasting the furious look in his eyes.

Garrett rubbed his jaw, not seeming to be seriously hurt. "I don't think you have much say about that, Tate. You already have a fiancé, remember? You have no claim on Rachel. Besides, it didn't seem to me as if she was objecting too much."

Dawson lunged for Garrett. Garrett dodged and managed to grab the garbage can before Dawson completely toppled in it.

Rachel had the strong urge to laugh. Dawson looked so ridiculously funny trying to attack Garrett while standing inside the garbage can.

"They're on to me!" Kelsey's voice bit across the feed, instantly ending the confrontation. "Head back out the kitchen entrance. But run! They're headed your way!"

"Dawson, get back in!" Rachel demanded. "Security knows Kelsey hacked in."

The elevator beeped their arrival at their destination as Dawson popped back in the can. Rachel and Garrett quickly piled the boxes back on top of him.

"I bet that man from downstairs decided to turn us in to our 'supervisor' after all," Garrett grumbled. "I knew this rescue was just too easy."

The doors slid open. Rachel and Garrett started running. Garrett was much faster and took over pushing the garbage can. Rachel was tempted to kick her heels off so she could run faster, but she was afraid she would need them again when they made it outside.

Employees swerved out of the way as Garrett barreled past. Through the hall. Past the supply room. Into the kitchen. Rachel could see the exit.

Almost there.

"They've spotted my van!" Kelsey's frantic voice came in Rachel's ear. "They'll be sending security out here. I have only a few minutes before I have to get away. You're on your own. I see about seven security guards closing in on your position. Get out! Get out!"

Chapter 11

Garrett slid to a stop. Two security men stood in between them and the door. Both Garrett and Rachel turned to go the other direction, automatically searching for a different escape route. About five more men, some uniformed, some not, stepped in back of them and tightened the circle. They were surrounded. There was no escape.

Garrett spoke from directly behind Rachel. "We have to get out of here. Time to see what you've actually got, Rachel."

"Just try to keep up, Garrett," Rachel gritted out.

Garrett moved forward. "I'm going to need to get out that door, boys."

"Go ahead and try," one of the men replied.

Rachel heard the unmistakable sound of a fist hitting flesh.

The two men in front of her advanced.

She didn't wait for an invitation. She kicked the knee of the man on the left. It was a perfect blow, hitting him right above the kneecap and slightly to the side. Before he even had time to react, she followed the kick up with a back-knuckle to the ear, right above his temple.

As he fell to the floor unconscious, she turned to the other man. Using her right leg, she planted another perfect kick to the knee, following it with a punch to the center of his forehead.

As he dropped like a sack of potatoes, someone grabbed Rachel from behind. His forearm locked right below her neck, and he started dragging her backward. Planting her feet, she jerked both arms up as high as fast as she could, loosening his hold. Simultaneously, she twisted slightly and raised her leg in a rear kick, planting her high heel directly into the inside of his thigh.

The man completely released his hold, bending over like he'd been kicked in the groin. He looked up at her, a murderous expression on his face. She quickly pivoted with a circular kick ending in a direct hit to his forehead. He crumpled to the floor unconscious.

Rachel movements had been seamless, flowing swiftly from one to another. All three attackers had taken Rachel less than thirty seconds total to dispose of. Garrett was still fighting the two men from the door. Dawson was out of the garbage can and struggling to defend himself against another security agent.

Spotting the lid from a pot on the counter, Rachel quickly picked it up and threw it like a Frisbee toward one of Garrett's attackers. It was a direct hit to the back of his head. Not waiting to make sure Garrett now had the advantage, she tore off in Dawson's direction. Dawson had just taken a hard punch to the gut. The security agent's back was to Rachel, and he was fumbling with grabbing some kind of weapon on his side. Knowing she had no time, Rachel spun around, arching her long leg in another perfect, circular, spinning heel kick and landing the side of her heel in a hard blow to the man's right temple. He dropped for what she knew would be a short nap, having never even seen her.

"Alright, that's enough, little lady."

Rachel heard a click and felt the unmistakable pressure of a gun barrel at her back. The seventh security agent. Immediately reacting, Rachel deliberately pushed her back against the gun, feeling the gun press hard and knowing it would loosen the man's grip. Stepping back with her right foot, she spun around and grabbed the man's gun hand with her right one. Before he knew what was happening,

Rachel had bent his hand back and now had the gun, though still in his hand, pointing directly at his own head.

"Go ahead. Shoot," Rachel said softly.

The man's mouth fell open in shock.

Reaching down to his hip, Rachel lifted the handcuffs dangling there. "Dawson, would you do the honors?"

While Dawson handcuffed him to the handle of one of the ovens, Rachel removed the guard's gun, phone, and walkie talkie and threw them in the garbage can. At some point, all of the white-shirted kitchen workers had cleared the premises. The five agents Rachel had disposed of lay motionless on the ground.

Garrett looked up, breathing hard, from where he had disposed of his two. "Come on! Let's get out of here before they send reinforcements!"

They all hurried into the warm night air and down the driveway. The gate began to close as they neared it. Thankfully, they were still able to slip through.

"Sorry, I can't wait for you," Kelsey's voice said. "I waited to make sure you made it through the gate, but I lost control of it right before you made it through. I've now got a security vehicle on my tail.

Security has already found your car, Garrett. You can't go back there"

"Just make sure you don't get caught, Kelsey," Garrett replied. "We'll figure something out. Call when you're safe."

Instead of continuing down the service driveway, Garrett changed directions and started cutting through the brush that fronted the house. If they had any hope of escaping, they had to find a different route. Worriedly she looked behind her at Dawson. He was following, plunging through the trees and bushes right behind them.

"Dawson you're moving better." Rachel whispered. Though he still had a significant limp, at least he was moving unassisted.

"Large amounts of adrenaline does wonders," he replied.

Branches grabbed at Rachel's hair and face. She struggled as her heels kept sinking in the mud. It was pitch black in the brush. She hoped Garrett had a better sense of direction than she did. She had no idea where they were or where they were headed, and the noise of them crashing through the foliage wasn't exactly subtle.

Finally, they burst into the open. They were in the parking lot filled with all the vehicles belonging to the party guests. Rachel could see Riley's house fully lit like a Christmas tree in the distance.

"How are you at stealing cars?" Garrett asked Dawson.

"Decent." Dawson replied. "Hot-wiring is easy, but it sometimes takes me a while to get into the car."

"Same here," Garrett said. "And we don't have any special equipment. But some makes are easier to break into than others. Maybe if we found the right type and worked together…"

As they discussed the details of a plan to steal a car, Rachel scanned the lot. There was a security van parked near the entrance to the parking lot where it met the street. A uniformed security guard stood outside. Thankfully, they still stood in the shadows and couldn't be seen.

"How about that older sedan over there?" Garrett was suggesting. "Now if we could just find some kind of tool."

Rachel rolled her eyes. Why did they have to go with the most complicated plan?

As the men continued to discuss the possibilities of finding a car with a slightly open window or simply trying to crack and break one, Rachel quickly removed the white shirt and pants of the kitchen scrubs and slid her black skirt back in place. She was not going to steal some poor person's car.

She pulled the remaining pins from her hair, shook it out, and turned to Garrett and Dawson.

"Alright guys, new plan. I'm going over to talk to that security guard by the entrance. All you have to do is get into position by the van without being seen. Be ready to jump in when I get the keys. Garrett, you're driving."

Garrett and Dawson looked at her with stunned expressions, but she didn't wait for a discussion. She confidently walked across the parking lot and sauntered directly up to the security guard.

His walkie talkie was in his hand and squawking a report, "… two men and a woman. The woman and one man are dressed in the white shirt and pants of kitchen workers."

"Okay, got it," the guard said. "I'll be on the lookout."

He slid the walkie talkie back into the case on his hip and turned around. Hoping her hair and makeup didn't look as scary as she feared, Rachel took a deep breath and gave what she hoped was a friendly, alluring smile.

"Hi, I was wondering if you could help me? I'm getting ready to leave, but I'm not familiar with the area and need some directions. Do you happen to have a map or a smart phone? I don't."

"Sure!" the security guard replied, his eyes lighting up and a goofy grin stretching his face. "Where do you need to go?"

"The Four Seasons in Miami," Rachel replied without hesitation. Thankfully, she had seen that one along with a bunch of other hotels when she and Garrett had driven to the bank.

"I can pull up a map right here," the guard said as he took out his phone and pushed a few buttons.

Rachel scooted close to his side as he began explaining and pointing at the map on the screen. She nodded and smiled like she was paying attention to every word he was saying.

Just a little closer!

Subtly pushing up against his side, she reached out and tried to carefully extract the ring of keys dangling on his hip. It was stuck!

She yanked. It still wouldn't come. Maybe if she twisted it to one side.

"What are you doing?" The guard said sharply, moving away from her side abruptly and turning to face her. Sudden wary suspicion clouded his previously friendly face.

Rachel sighed. "I was trying to swipe your keys, but obviously, since that's not working…"

Rachel quickly raised her hand like a blade and brought it down in a karate-chop motion right at the base of his neck, where the neck and the shoulder meet. It was a hard hit. Instantly, it was as if the man's right leg had turned to jelly. He collapsed. Rachel quickly removed his cell phone and walkie talkie, tossing them a few feet away. This time when she grabbed the keys, they came easily.

The guard looked up at her from the pavement, his eyes wide and his mouth moving as if trying to form words.

"Just relax," Rachel urged. "You'll be able to move your right side in about twenty minutes."

Rachel turned, ran to the security van, and hopped in the passenger's side. Garrett and Dawson were already inside. She handed Garrett the keys. He took them, but paused, staring at Rachel with an open mouth.

"Who ARE you?" he asked.

"Just drive!" Rachel ordered.

Garrett obediently put the keys in the ignition, started the van, and took off, but he kept glancing at Rachel with an incredulous look on his face.

After only about a minute, Garrett spoke again. "Okay, Rachel. Back there in the kitchen, I'm pretty sure I saw you take out five guys in less than two minutes. Plus, you also managed to assist me by throwing a pan lid into the back of one guy's head. I didn't have a great view, since I was already busy, but I did catch your movements out of the corner of my eye. By the time I got my two down, everyone else was on the floor. Now, you managed to drop a guy with a single blow. So, either you're some kind of highly trained secret government agent or my dream girl come to life, maybe both."

Dawson snorted from the back seat. "Sorry. Wrong on both counts, Garrett. Her dad taught her."

"Your dad?" Garrett asked. "How? Was he an agent or something?"

"No," Dawson replied. "He's just one ordinary, dangerous, thoroughly awesome guy. You really wouldn't want to try to pull anything on him. He was a sharpshooter in the military when he was younger and, at some point, was apparently befriended by a Chinese guy who taught him martial arts. He, in turn, taught Rachel everything. But, he readily admits Rachel took everything he taught her and took it to the next level. She's always been gifted. Her dad said he thinks she was really a child prodigy when it came to things like weaponry and martial arts."

Rachel made a face. "But obviously, pick-pocketing wasn't part of my education."

"It certainly didn't look like it needed to be," Garrett said.

Rachel glanced over at the speedometer. Garrett was carefully adhering to the speed limit, apparently trying to take advantage of their incognito transportation and not attract attention in their escape. While she understood, it was maddening to feel like they were crawling at a snail's pace when all her nerves were screaming at Garrett to step on it.

"How did you drop him with one blow like that?" Garrett asked.

Rachel shrugged. "It was just a nerve strike that my dad showed me. If you can hit it right, the person will be completely paralyzed on one side for about twenty minutes. I would have rather not hurt the guy at all, but at least he won't have any lingering effects."

Garrett took his eyes off the road and flashed Rachel a look of utter admiration. "You're dangerous."

Somehow, Rachel didn't think he was talking solely about her ability to thoroughly beat up an attacker.

Rachel could feel the anger and tension radiating from Dawson in the back seat.

"So, are we headed back to the office?" Rachel asked, wanting to ease the tension and get back on task.

"No," Dawson said. "We can't. At least, not yet."

"Why not?" Rachel asked. She watched as Garrett's eyes met Dawson's in the rearview mirror.

"He doesn't have any evidence against John Riley," Garrett replied. "Until we have something concrete, we are still considered a rogue mission with no affiliation to Homeland Security. We will get no protection and no help from them."

"But Dawson was kidnapped!" Rachel said. "Isn't that evidence enough against John Riley?"

"I never saw Riley," Dawson said. "He was never even mentioned. It was other men who jumped me, knocked me out, and then later questioned me. They definitely wanted to know what I had on Riley, but his name was never mentioned."

"But you were imprisoned in his house!"

"That's not enough," Dawson said. "That's insignificant–like peanuts if compared to the charges we want to get Riley on."

Garrett took over. "Plus, since there is no evidence of affiliation to Riley, other than the house, it would be very easy for Riley to pawn the kidnapping off on a scapegoat. We would lose every possibility of getting near enough to find solid evidence on him. Everything Dawson has worked for would be wasted."

"So, what do we do?" Rachel asked. "How long do we have to hide out?"

Garrett glanced back at Dawson. "That's your call, Dawson. In the file Rachel got from the safety deposit box, you indicated you were very close to some hard evidence. So where is it, and how do we get our hands on it ASAP?"

Rachel had turned around in her seat to look at Dawson. When Garrett mentioned that Rachel had located the safety deposit box, Dawson's eyes flashed to her, and he smiled briefly, as if to say, 'Good girl, Rachel.' Rachel ignored him and deliberately turned back around. Now that he was safe and the immediate danger had passed, she was once again feeling heavy doses of hurt and anger toward the man she had thought she loved.

"I'm scheduled to meet my informant tomorrow morning," Rachel heard Dawson say. "He's supposed to give me the evidence I need against Riley. I'll have to make that meeting. I originally had it scheduled for Wednesday night, when I first arrived here in Miami. But my informant is deservedly nervous. He called at the last minute, saying he'd have to meet me Saturday morning instead. That was right before I was jumped by a bunch of thugs and drugged with something. Now, since my cell phone was taken and I can't use it, I have no way of contacting him to even make sure he'll be there."

"We found your phone," Garrett said. "But it's at the office. Couldn't you just use a different phone? Don't you have his number?"

"We used a code when texting. If he sees the code coming from a different number, he'll panic and disappear. He can't know that I was kidnapped. There's nothing I can do except go to the designated place tomorrow morning and hope he shows up."

"So we'll have to hole up somewhere until tomorrow morning," Garrett said thoughtfully. "But the first thing we need to do is ditch this security van. Sorry, Rachel, you were awesome to snag this van and get us out of there, but it's too easy to track. We're going to need some other transportation if we want to thoroughly disappear."

"Speaking of which, I think we've got a problem," Dawson said. "There's a car a couple lengths back that's been following us for the past five minutes."

"I've noticed it too," Garrett said. "It makes every turn I do, but never gets any closer. Why is that? If it's Riley's men, why aren't they trying to stop us?

Rachel looked out her side view mirror. She saw the pair of headlights they were talking about, but they were so far back, she would have never even noticed if they were following.

There was so much distance between the two vehicles that, as Rachel watched, another vehicle turned and took its place behind the security van. Suddenly bright lights lit like Christmas, and the sound of a loud siren made Rachel practically jump out of her skin.

"The police!" Rachel shrieked.

Chapter 12

"Great, that's all we need," Garrett muttered, making no move to pull over and yet not increasing the pressure of his foot on the gas.

"Are you already speeding or something, Garrett?" Rachel questioned. "Why are they after us?"

"Because we broke into Riley's house and stole a security van!" Garrett bit back. "That's why they're after us! And, no, I am not speeding, at least for the moment."

"But that doesn't make sense," Rachel protested. "Why would Riley call the police on us? I wouldn't think he'd want them involved."

"Why not?" Dawson said quietly from the back. "We have no evidence. Riley has nothing to lose. Option one, we are apprehended by the police and there is a huge scandal implicating us and Homeland Security in unlawful breaking and entering and grand theft. Option two, the cops chase us, but Riley's men do the actual apprehending. Who knows, maybe Riley even has some dirty cops on the force. Calling the police makes Riley appear more honest and forthright and eliminates the problem of us. It's a win-win situation. The only option not permissible is allowing us to escape. Bringing in the cops now doubles the number of people searching for us."

Rachel felt a surreal sense of déjà vu. She'd been involved in a car chase at night before. It had ended with her and Dawson's car being smashed into a warehouse. She did not want to do that again.

Rachel's phone beeped. She fumbled to open it.

"Hello?"

"Hi, it's Kelsey. You guys are in trouble. Riley reported you to the police."

"Yeah, we kind of already figured that out. Especially since we are being chased right now! And right behind the police are Riley's men!"

"Listen carefully, Rachel. You do not have authorization to do anything to the police officers or their car. Your only option is to escape."

Rachel relayed the message to Garrett and Dawson.

"That's exactly why I'm not putting to good use every technique I learned in evasive driving!"

Garrett said. Rachel lifted the phone and put it on speaker so Kelsey could hear him speaking. "If we have a full-blown chase, somebody could get hurt, including the police or civilians. But, if we wait too long, the police will call in reinforcements and set up a blockade. So, do you have any great ideas, Kelsey? How am I going to lose both the police and Riley's men when I can't do anything that might cause potential collateral damage?"

"Yes, as a matter of fact, I do. I've already talked to Andrews and have obtained an unmarked car. You just have to lose your entourage, dump the security van, and make the switch."

"That sounds easy enough," Garrett said sarcastically.

Ignoring him, Kelsey continued, "I'm tracking your location. There is a parking garage about two minutes away. Follow my directions, and I'll get you there. Maintain your speed until I tell you, then you'll have about twenty seconds to hit it hard, make several sharp turns, and pull into the parking garage without your followers seeing."

"Sounds fun," Garrett said. "Lead on."

Garrett obediently followed Kelsey's instructions, keeping the van at a very sedate pace. Two minutes seemed like ten to Rachel. At any second, she kept expecting to see more police cruisers in front of them, trapping them and eliminating all escape. The piercing sirens screamed after them, surrounding Rachel in a living nightmare and raking across her nerves like gasoline being poured onto an already blazing fire.

Garrett turned a corner.

"Okay, Garrett, hit it!" Kelsey said, her words now coming rapidly as she instructed him in several sharp turns.

The tires screeched around the corners, throwing Rachel to one side and then the other. It felt like they were going in circles. Rachel had enough trouble trying to keep track of which end was up; she had no clue if they were being successful at eluding their pursuers.

Garrett finally took a sharp right, then another sharp right into a parking garage. He pulled up the ramp and into a shadowy empty parking space in the midst of a group of other vehicles. He shut off the engine. They were all silent, waiting. From their position a little higher than the street, they still had a partial view of the front entrance. Rachel could hear both Garrett and Dawson's heavy breathing in the suddenly hushed interior. She was desperately trying to shake off her dizziness to focus on the entrance.

Had they done it? Had they escaped both the police and Riley's men?

The police cruiser sped past, lights and sirens still blaring.

Then... nothing.

As the seconds ticked by, Rachel felt herself starting to breathe again. The police had been in front of the other car. If they hadn't caught sight of their escape, then it was unlikely that...

A dark sedan passed slowly in front of the garage. It turned in the front entrance.

"Get out!" Kelsey yelled, still on speaker phone.

Rachel fumbled with the door handle, jerking it open and sliding to the pavement. They were going to get caught! There was no way Riley's men would miss the security van.

Crouching low, Rachel made her way to the front of the van. She could hear the engine of a vehicle coming closer slowly, then stopping directly behind the van. The cell phone was still in her hand. She fumbled to turn it off speaker and then pressed it to her ear.

"How do we get out of here, Kelsey?' she whispered.

As she met up with the other two men by the hood of the van, Kelsey responded. "There is a stairwell a few yards back toward the front entrance. It exits at the side of the building on the street level.

I left the keys in the car for you. It's a gray Honda. But remember, you can't let them see you in the new car. If they can track it, then everything we've done is pointless."

Rachel hung up the phone with Kelsey and whispered the message to Garrett and Dawson.

That's when the gunshots started. A few bullets whizzed above their heads, giving an added danger as they hit the concrete.

"Guess they've given up on trying to take us alive," Garrett muttered. "And what's worse, they don't appear to be the brightest of bad guys."

Rachel understood what he meant as she watched the bullets ricochet off the cement walls. The shooters were just as likely to hit themselves with a stray bullet as they were to hit their target.

"How many of them are there?" Rachel asked quietly.

"I counted four," Garrett replied. "But given our position and the fact that they're trigger happy, I wouldn't recommend trying to take them out."

"We need some kind of distraction," Dawson said. "That's the only way we're going to get out of here alive and unseen."

"I left the van in neutral," Garrett said with a grin. "If we give it a good push, it will probably keep rolling right into their fancy car parked behind."

"That might work for a distraction," Dawson said, "but there probably wouldn't be much damage to the car. I would feel better about it if I knew for sure they wouldn't be able to follow us. Do either of you have a gun?"

Garret replied, "No, we weren't authorized… Wait a minute! Rachel, didn't you say you were bringing that little gun?"

"The Walther?" Dawson asked

Rachel nodded. " I have it."

Dawson grinned. "Perfect. Rachel, do you think you can manage to shoot a couple of their tires out?"

After the initial barrage of bullets, Riley's men had stopped firing, seeming to realize the danger to themselves. The light in the parking garage was dim. With it being pitch black outside, the only light source was from the white fluorescent lights situated periodically at intervals along the ceiling. But, at least it would be a very close shot.

"Sure," she said. "I can get the two closest to us."

"Are you sure?" Garrett asked, obviously hesitant. "Maybe I should be the one to make the shot. You haven't been through training yet."

"No," Dawson said, grinning. "Trust me. We want her to do the shooting."

Garrett shrugged as if he still wasn't convinced, but he wasn't going to argue.

"Okay, people!" A voice echoed from the other side of the van. "We're going to give you exactly thirty seconds to come out with your hands where we can see them. If you decide not to join us, we're coming in after you."

"They're going to try to surround us!" Garrett said.

"Now, Rachel!" Dawson urged. "Do it now!"

Wasting no time, Rachel hiked up her dress and removed the small gun from her calf. Laying on the concrete, she peeked around the side of the van, took aim, and fired. Sitting up, Garrett and Dawson got out of her way as she then crawled to the other side of the van, calmly repeating the procedure with the other tire.

By the sound of the angry cursing at the other end of the van, Rachel and everyone else were fully assured that her shots had hit their marks.

Garrett and Dawson began pushing the van backward. Rachel added her strength and, within a few feet, they had it rolling nicely. They released it to the tune of the surprised, frantic yells of their would-be pursuers.

The three agents didn't wait for results. As soon as their fingers parted from the front of the van, they took off running along the narrow strip of space fronting the parked cars. This time, Rachel gladly left her heels, her bare feet padding soundlessly as she sprinted for the exit.

The crunch of metal on metal barely registered as Rachel saw the Exit sign ahead. They bypassed the elevator and scurried straight for the stairs. Unfortunately, bright fluorescent lights fully illuminated the steps. As her feet flew lightly down the cold cement stairs, she braced herself, expecting bullets to echo through the stairwell at any second. Her breathing sounded loud in the hollow space. Almost there. Just a few more steps

Rachel was right behind Garrett as they reached the door to the outside. Dawson emerged mere seconds after her.

Immediately in front of them was the gray Honda. Garrett took the driver's seat while Rachel took the back. For once, she didn't mind giving up the shotgun position to Dawson.

As Garrett turned the keys in the ignition, Rachel looked back.

Had they been followed?

But the glow of the streetlights revealed only the empty street.

As Garrett pulled away from the curb, Rachel continued to watch behind them. They turned a corner, then another. Everyone in the car seemed to be holding their breath, waiting for the headlights to appear behind them. Yet the late-night streets behind them remained deserted. As Garrett turned onto increasingly busy streets, other cars filled up the streets, and yet none of them followed on Garrett's complex maze of a route.

Rachel's phone rang.

"Looks like you guys made it," Kelsey said as Rachel pushed the speaker button. "As far as I can tell, Riley's men are still stuck in the parking garage."

"Thanks for your help, Kelsey," Dawson said.

"No problem. Sorry I didn't stay and join your party, but I figured I would be able to help you better from afar. Besides, none of Riley's men saw me."

"You're right. We need you to run interference," Garrett said.

"Do you know where you're headed?" Kelsey asked.

"I've got a pretty good idea where we can hole up for the night," Dawson answered. "We'll give you a call when we get there. We'll meet my informant tomorrow morning and hopefully get the evidence on Riley. Then we can end this mess."

"Sounds good. I'll keep Andrews in the loop."

The call ended.

As Dawson and Garrett discussed where they were headed, Rachel leaned her head back, tuning them out. Her muscles began releasing the tension from the past few hours. Finally, she felt like she could breathe. They were going to make it. At least for the next few hours, they were safe.

A warm fog settled over Rachel. Sometime later, she became aware that she had fallen asleep, yet her brain was still listening and recording everything that was going on around her. The hard seat back, the motion of the moving car, the quiet conversation of the men in the front seats.

"We're almost to the hotel. I guess we should wake Rachel."

Rachel recognized Dawson's voice.

"No, let her sleep," came Garrett's reply. "I think she's been awake for nearing forty-eight hours. From what I understand, she took the first flight she could get out of Montana. It was a red-eye that landed in Miami this morning. Then she immediately began working on finding you. Leave her alone. She's earned the rest."

Rachel felt the car stop and heard one of the doors open and shut as one of the men left. She tried to rouse herself. She wanted to see where they were, but it was as if her body wouldn't obey. Instead, she dozed into a deeper sleep.

The sound of the car door once again parted the fog.

"Okay, we're registered under an alias for room 209." Garrett said. "It's upstairs. They didn't have any more rooms on the ground floor. I'll just carry Rachel up if you can get the door."

"No," Dawson replied. "I'll carry Rachel. You can get the door."

"Look. You're obviously in no condition to carry her. You'd probably end up injuring yourself and her. I'll do it."

"There's no way I'm going to let you carry my girlfriend up those stairs!"

Their argument stopped at the sound of the opening car door.

Rachel leaned back inside the Honda. "You guys can sit in here and argue all you want. I'll be in room 209."

She slammed the door. *Men and their stupid egos! I have two legs; they could have just woken me up! But no! They had to sit there and argue about who was going to CARRY me!*

By the time she had reached the exterior stairs of the second-rate hotel, both Garrett and Dawson were at her heels. She started up the steps, still fuming. About the fifth stair up, her vision started to black out. Her muscles suddenly seemed as if they could no longer carry her weight. She swayed, grabbing for the railing. Her fingers slid off the metal. She felt herself falling.

Strong arms caught her and swung her easily up into a cradled position. Garrett.

"Not a word, Dawson," Garrett said firmly. "Not a single word."

"Put me down, Garrett!" Rachel protested, her voice sounding strangely weak, even to her own ears. "I can do it…"

"Rachel!" Dawson said sharply. "Just for once, let someone do something for you!"

Feeling too weak to argue, Rachel closed her eyes and leaned her head against Garrett. "I don't know what's wrong with me," she mumbled.

"Your body's shutting down because of exhaustion," Garrett said gently. "Don't worry. You'll be ready to beat me up again tomorrow."

Rachel finally gave up and relaxed in Garrett's arms, putting her arms securely around his neck. It was a strange sensation to feel almost weightless as she was effortlessly carried up the stairs and across the landing. She could feel the warmth of his skin against her cheek; smell the slightly musky, masculine scent that surrounds him. She felt safe.

She liked the way she felt in his arms and didn't want it to end. All too soon, they were in the hotel room, and he was placing her gently on a bed. As he released her, Rachel grabbed his hand. She tried to thank him, but couldn't seem to form the words with her mouth. She looked up at him. The room was dark, and yet his eyes were darker still.

Giving up, she let sleep finally take her. The last thing she remembered was feeling a soft, loving caress trail along her cheek.

Chapter 13

"Rachel."

Dawson's voice reached out, gently but forcibly pulling her from the deep warm darkness.

She opened her eyes.

"Hey, Montana," Dawson said, smiling gently. "Time to wake up. Garrett's in the shower. After he's done, it'll be your turn, and then we have to go meet my informant. It's early. Sorry I couldn't let you sleep longer."

Rachel sat up, a bit unnerved that she had been so oblivious for the past few hours.

"That's okay," Rachel replied, looking around the room. It was clean, but simply furnished. This was obviously a hotel meant for the budget-conscious and not meant for luxury, which was perfectly fine with Rachel.

She looked back at Dawson. He looked terrible. He and Garrett must have taken turns keeping watch. But more than the exhaustion, his eyes appeared haunted.

"Montana, we need to talk. I know I have a lot to explain."

A sudden, intense wave of hurt and anger rolled over Rachel as she remembered everything. But, now, all the questions seemed pointless.

"I don't know that there is anything to say," Rachel said. "You're engaged to Vanessa. End of story. I just don't understand why you lied to me and made me believe we had a relationship."

"No, Rachel. You have it wrong. Vanessa was an asset. I had to use her to get information on her father." He took a deep breath and ran a hand through his hair, as if struggling to find the words. "Vanessa is my girlfriend from way back. After the attempted terrorist bombing in New York, we suspected that there might be an American connection. Meaning, it didn't appear to be an entirely overseas operation. We thought there might be an influential American funding and enabling the terrorist ring."

"The terrorists had no accents," Rachel said, remembering both that night in New York and her previous conversation with Andrews.

"Exactly," Dawson replied. "Many of the terrorists we ran into and later apprehended spoke like Americans, not Middle Eastern extremists. That was one of the clues. Then, when we investigated them, we found out that they actually were Americans! Though we got very little intel on who hired them. Although I had been promoted, Andrews assigned me the case of investigating several suspects, including Riley. I recognized his name as my ex-girlfriend's father. I knew then that I didn't have a choice. I was in the unique position where I already had a relationship with Vanessa that would provide the perfect cover."

"But you could have told me!"

"No, I couldn't! It was top secret! Besides, would you have really been okay with me telling you I was going to romance another woman for the sake of my investigation?"

"But on some level it was apparently okay for me to know. You obviously intended to draw me into the investigation if something should ever happen to you. Andrews called me your failsafe."

"No." Dawson shook his head adamantly. "I never intended to involve you. I didn't want to put you at risk if not absolutely necessary. That's why I put the file in the safety deposit box and didn't tell you. I had a program set up that if I didn't put in a code at a certain time, an automatic text with that address would be sent to you. You also have an email in your inbox with the same address. I assumed you would get the file and immediately give it to Andrews. I certainly didn't expect you to get involved. And I didn't expect Andrews to allow it. I put the gun in there for your protection. Knowing any small detail about this investigation would put you at risk."

"But none of that changes the fact that you lied to me about Vanessa, about everything. And don't you dare tell me you didn't. A lie of omission is still a lie. I just don't understand. You said you were a Christian. Were you just pretending for my sake? How can you be a Christian and be so deceptive?"

Dawson's eyes reflected hurt. "Rachel, everything in my relationship with you was true. Everything I said, every feeling, everything we did together; that was real. I am a Christian. But my job is to protect my country. Sometimes I have to do things that would otherwise be wrong in order to fulfill that duty. Biblically, think about the spies who were sent into Canaan. Remember how Rahab lied to protect them? Were the spies wrong for spying? Was Rahab wrong for lying? No. There are certain instances where I believe lying is okay in order to protect the welfare of others. If someone came in here determined to hurt or kill you, I would lie through my teeth and say you weren't here. The greater sin would be to tell the truth and enable them to hurt you. In the case of my job, I sometimes have to lie in an effort to protect an entire country of innocent people. I don't like it, but I do it anyway. Does that make sense?"

Rachel closed her eyes, trying to think. "Dawson, I know you've obviously given this a lot of thought. But the problem is that, in your case, your professional and personal life intersect. Your own parents don't even know the truth of what you do. They think you own a security company, and they are expecting you to marry Vanessa Riley! How am I supposed to know what the truth with you even is?

Dawson winced. "Originally, I didn't tell my parents I worked for Homeland Security because I didn't want to worry my mom. Then, I guess, the lie became convenient to my work. I've had the front of a security company for years. The agency knows about it and helps me to fully maintain the cover. When I had to renew my relationship with Vanessa, my parents got involved. They knew Vanessa from previously. There was no way to keep them out of it."

"Even if I understand and accept everything you've told me, Dawson, I can't accept that you're *engaged* to her! Isn't that going a little beyond the call of duty? Romancing her, getting close to her to get information on her father is one thing, but asking her to *marry* you?"

"For the record, I never proposed to Vanessa. She pretty much told me we were getting married or the relationship was over. At that point, I was so very close to getting some hard evidence on her father, I felt like I had to go through with it."

"So were you going to go through with marrying her, too? You're scheduled to marry her in what, six weeks? I attended your engagement party last night. It was nice. Sorry you missed it." Rachel knew she was sounding sarcastic and bitter, but she felt helpless to stop.

"I never intended on marrying her, Rachel." Dawson's deep blue eyes begged her to understand. "And, as soon as we arrest Riley, I'll tell her so, and the fake relationship will be over."

"Oh, that's nice of you. Arrest her dad and break her heart in the same day? That'll crush her!" Acid dripped from her voice. Rachel wasn't normally so vicious, but the anger and hurt was overwhelming. Everything Dawson said only seemed to make it worse. "I still don't understand how you can be okay with using people like that and then cruelly tossing them aside."

"Vanessa won't be hurt, Rachel."

It was somewhat aggravating to Rachel to realize that Dawson's voice remained soft and calm, despite her anger. Even now, his tone was humble but confident as he tried to reassure her.

"She may come across as very sweet," Dawson continued, "but she is actually very conniving. She is not a nice person. Honestly, my parents will probably be very relieved when I tell them we're not getting married. They've never liked her. There was a time I strongly suspected Vanessa of being involved with her father's illegal dealings. She's certainly capable, but I never found any evidence. Don't worry about Vanessa. She doesn't love me. She was using me as much as I was using her."

"If she didn't love you, why did she want to marry you?"

Dawson sighed. "The Rileys are under the impression that I'm very wealthy and have extensive international connections through my business. They thought it would be a good match professionally. I'm sure Vanessa has some feelings for me. She likes me and was tired of waiting for our relationship to go to the next level. But she doesn't love me."

Rachel was quiet a moment. Finally, some of the red hot anger seemed to be dissipating, leaving only raw, suffocating hurt. She spoke, her voice barely above a whisper. "I still don't know what to believe. Is what you are telling me now the truth, or is it just another cover for another mission?"

Dawson looked almost sick at her words, his gaze faltering then raising back up to anxiously search her eyes. "Everything I'm telling you is the truth, Rachel. Everything in our relationship was and is the truth. Anything you want to know, any detail about me, ask me now, Rachel, and I'll tell you the truth. Ask me anything. Ask me now."

"Did you sleep with Vanessa?"

"No. Never. She always knew I was a Christian and knew my convictions. She didn't like them or share them, but I didn't compromise. I am the same man wherever I am, Rachel. I just had a cover."

"Did you tell her you loved her?"

He paused. His blue eyes were so sincere, so honest.

"Yes, I did," he said, holding Rachel's gaze steady. "I lied."

And that was probably the one detail she couldn't live with. For the first time, Rachel felt her eyes fill with tears. He had never even hinted that he loved Rachel, yet he had apparently effortlessly swore his love to Vanessa Riley.

She swallowed, trying to choke down the knot in her throat. She would not let him see her cry.

"I'm sorry, Dawson," she said, her voice strained. "I just don't think we can have a relationship anymore. I still don't believe that you truly cared for me, or cared about me enough. How could you tell one woman you loved her if you cared about another? Even if we were to try to salvage something, I would never know if you were telling me the truth. What happens next time Andrews assigns you a case that involves an 'asset?' I'll always wonder if you're off romancing someone else. I can't count on anything you say to me as being true. If you feel for any reason that something intersects your job or an investigation in any way, you'll lie to me. Bottom line, I don't trust you. And I never will."

Dawson stared at Rachel, his beautiful deep blue eyes seeming to search her very soul. She didn't waver.

"I can't accept that," he whispered. "I'm not willing to let you go, Montana. Can't you see, you're the only thing in my life that *is* real!"

The bathroom door opened, and Garrett walked out.

"Your turn, Rachel!" he said cheerfully. Then stopping, he looked from Rachel's obviously upset face to Dawson's. "Well, I take it that went well. Oh well, live and learn, Dawson. Rachel, you better hurry if you want a shower before we leave. Kelsey's going to meet us there, and we still have quite a few preparations to make."

Without a word, Rachel got up from the bed, walked into the bathroom, and shut the door.

Chapter 14

The tension between Garrett and Dawson was thick as they drove to meet with Dawson's informant. As Rachel had come out of the bathroom, she had heard their angry voices. But when they saw her, they had immediately stopped. She could only assume they had been arguing about her.

"Did you call Kelsey?" Garrett asked Dawson.

Apparently, they were trying to keep everything professional and not discuss what was really charging the air between them.

"Yes. I talked to her right as we were leaving. She'll meet us there."

"The meeting place hasn't changed since last night, has it?" Rachel asked. "Why didn't you tell Kelsey sooner?" She knew their hotel was relatively close to the meeting point. But what if Kelsey couldn't make it there on such short notice?

"Because he's paranoid." Garrett replied smugly.

"Yes, I am paranoid," Dawson snapped back. "And besides that, I don't trust anybody. The less people who know about this meeting, the better. If Kelsey knew the location, she would have had to tell Andrews. And, there's a chance that, with obtaining such volatile information, he would have insisted on a full team to monitor the meet. One glimpse of something unusual, and my informant will take off. Also, there's the chance that Riley has connections within the DEA or Homeland Security. The less people know about the meet and location, the less chance that Riley will find out and prevent it."

They pulled up beside some kind of warehouse. Kelsey was already there and waiting outside her car."

"How did Andrews take the news?" Dawson asked.

"About as you would expect," Kelsey replied. "He was not happy about the short notice. He himself will be arriving with a team the minute you obtain the evidence. He wanted to be here sooner, but I talked him into holding off since your informant is so nervous. We're to give him updates practically every minute."

"Okay, do you have the equipment?" Dawson asked. "We have just enough time to get in position before he arrives."

Asking Kelsey if she was prepared was a pretty stupid question. Rachel was learning that Kelsey always seemed to think of everything. She'd even magically managed to have Rachel's suitcase waiting for her at the hotel when she woke up this morning. Just having clean clothes was enough to earn Rachel's undying devotion. Dawson and Garrett were right. If you needed someone to be doing the background legwork on a mission, Kelsey was obviously the best.

Kelsey began unloading her car and handing things to Garrett. Dawson, obviously the one calling the shots on this mission, began quickly outlining the plan.

"The meeting will take place right in front of that warehouse," he said, pointing to a large barn-like structure. There was a large opening at the front, as if, at least the ground level of the warehouse was typically used as a garage for large vehicles. "Should be a good location. Lots of open space. Not a lot of risky hiding places since the warehouse itself is open. But that also means you guys will have to take to the roofs to be hidden and still provide protection in case something unexpected happens."

"Kelsey, I figured you would be stationed over there," he said, pointing to a spot on the roof of a neighboring warehouse to the right."

"Rachel, you and Garrett will be over there," he said, pointing to a building to the left. "It's a little further away, but it will provide a slightly different angle and a better view of anyone approaching. Any questions?"

At their silence, Kelsey handed Garrett one of two sniper rifles. Rachel recognized it as a fully equipped M48 sniper rifle.

"Are you sure you don't want to take a weapon, Dawson?" Kelsey asked.

"No, I'd better not. This guy will spook very easily. With my luck, he'll insist on searching me before giving me the evidence. I'm already taking a risk by carrying the wire, but it's small enough it won't be noticeable unless he knew what he was looking for."

"Okay, we're all set then," Kelsey announced, taking the other sniper rifle.

"Wait a minute, where's mine?" Rachel asked, looking between Garrett and Kelsey.

"Sorry, Rachel," Garret replied. "You haven't gone through training and qualified on this weapon. We can't give one to you. It's against the rules. Here you go."

He handed her a pair of binoculars.

"I'm the lookout?" she said, incredulous.

"Don't be offended, Rachel," Garrett said. "We need you. And the lookout is probably the most important position."

Rachel rolled her eyes at his attempt to pacify her. She didn't want the binoculars like she was in the junior division. She wanted a gun.

Garrett and Kelsey moved to take their positions.

Dawson came up behind Rachel and cupped his hands on her shoulders. Leaning in, he whispered in her ear, his breath sending tickles all the way down her spine. "If it were up to me, you would have been first to have a gun."

Rachel froze. Dawson's breath moved from her ear to her neck. Goosebumps pricked over her entire body, and her breathing became shallow. The feather-light touch of lips on her neck electrified every nerve in her body. Rachel jumped. Spinning out of his hold, she glared into his dancing eyes.

The evil man! He had always known the physical effect he had on her. Apparently, he'd meant what he said about not being willing to let her go. And now, he was making it obvious that he was willing to use whatever means necessary to change her mind.

Dawson's gorgeous dimples made an appearance with the ornery grin that spread across his face. Rachel backed away. Without a word, she turned and ran to catch up with Garrett, choosing to completely ignore the delighted laughter behind her.

Rachel and Garrett took their position on the roof. Rachel could see Dawson below in front of the warehouse. While Garrett sighted in the rifle and made sure he had a good angle, Rachel sighed, took up the binoculars, and scanned the area. There were a lot of warehouses in this area and most of them seemed deserted this Saturday morning.

"Rachel, do you think you could teach me some of those nerve strikes you were doing yesterday," Garrett asked conversationally. "At the top of my list to learn is the one you used on the security guard."

"Sure," Rachel replied. Suddenly, in the silence, Rachel felt Garrett's eyes on her. Removing the binoculars, she turned to find him studying her, his gray gaze intense.

"Dawson is an absolute idiot to even risk losing you," he said softly. "I wouldn't make that mistake."

His gaze held her. She couldn't look away. The air between them suddenly became charged and Rachel remembered the feel of his lips on hers in the dark room of Riley's basement. Garrett stepped forward. She saw his gaze shift to her lips. She wanted him to kiss her–to just for a moment escape into that heart-pounding passion.

Suddenly coming to her senses, she shook her head slightly and stepped back. What was she thinking? Just a few moments ago she had felt an intense attraction for Dawson, and now she was longing for Garrett to kiss her? What kind of woman was she? How was it possible for her to have such feelings for two men at the same time? The only thing she knew for sure was that she couldn't trust herself or her feelings right now.

"Garrett, I'm really messed up right now. I'm not in any shape to be in a relationship. I barely know up from down. It wouldn't be fair to you to start something when I can't even trust myself."

Garrett nodded, looking away, and picking up his weapon once more. "I understand, Rachel. But, at the same time, I think it's only fair to warn you. I'm not a patient man. I see what I want and I go after it." Once again, he caught her gaze and held it. "And I've decided I want you."

Rachel didn't know how to respond. She really didn't want to be caught in the middle between two men, especially when both were incredibly handsome and drew her like a moth caught between two flames.

Looking away, she once again brought the binoculars up to her eyes. Maybe things would take care of themselves, and she wouldn't have to worry about it. It was unlikely that Garrett's interest in her would continue after this investigation. And Dawson would get the hint when she told him he needed to remove his things from her parents' guest house in Montana. Realistically, she didn't imagine continuing any kind of relationship with either man after things were wrapped up here in Miami.

"Here comes a car," Rachel announced.

Garrett rummaged through a bag and handed her one of the wires and earpieces he had gotten from Kelsey.

"We should have probably put these on a few minutes ago," Garrett said. "Dawson and Kelsey are probably having a fit."

"Sorry, guys," he said once the pieces were in place. "We're in position and have a car approaching slowly from the west."

"Color?" Dawson asked.

"Dark blue," Rachel replied. "Looks like an older model compact car, but you know I'm not good at identifying make and model."

"That's him," Dawson confirmed. "Garrett and Kelsey, do both of you have a good line of sight?"

At their confirmation, he continued. "Okay, let's make this exchange quick."

"I see only one occupant in the car," Rachel reported.

"So far, so good," Dawson muttered as the car pulled up.

A short, balding man with glasses got out the car. He reminded Rachel of a nervous little bird as his head moved every which way, scanning the area. She felt she could probably see him twitching and shaking even without the binoculars.

"Do you have it?" Dawson asked him.

"Yes, but I think Riley might be on to me," the man said, his voice high pitched and squeaking in his agitation.

"We can arrange to get you some protection after we arrest Riley, or before if you prefer," Dawson said.

"No, no. Definitely not before. I don't want to arouse any suspicion if I'm wrong."

"The sooner we have the evidence, the sooner we can arrest Riley and this will all be over," Dawson said in a soothing voice.

"Uh, I think we have a problem," Rachel said. "I see a dark SUV approaching rapidly.

"Are they our guys?" Garrett asked.

Rachel flipped back to see the informant hand Dawson a large manila envelope. Dawson wasted no time in ushering him back toward the car, but they never made it.

The dark SUV pulled in right in front of them, blocking their escape. Three men got out.

"They aren't our guys!" Kelsey yelled. "Andrews says they aren't ours! They've got to be Riley's men. We are authorized to use whatever means necessary to secure the evidence!"

But it was too late.

Rachel watched in horror as the three men, with weapons drawn, pushed Dawson and his informant into the large opening of the warehouse. Rachel realized that, with the position of the SUV and the cover of the warehouse, Garrett's line of sight was completely gone.

"I don't have the shot!" Garrett said, frustration evident. "Kelsey, shoot! Take them out!"

"My line of sight is gone!" Kelsey's voice reported urgently. "I have no shot! I'm calling Andrews for backup!"

Rachel scanned the area, frantic. What were they going to do? They didn't have time to wait for reinforcements!

One of the men, apparently the leader, pushed further into the warehouse. The other two men stayed at the front as if on guard for interruption. Garrett and Kelsey could probably maneuver around and get decent shots at the men in front, but that would do no good. Dawson and the informant would be dead and the third man probably gone in the SUV with the evidence before they could get a shot at him. No, they had to take out the leader first.

As if from a nightmare, she heard the hoarse voice of one of Riley's men. "I think you have something that belongs to us, Tate. I'll be taking it off your hands now."

"No, thanks," came Dawson's reply. "I think I'd rather keep it, if you don't mind."

Dawson was stalling. But for what? Their hands were tied.

Garrett was rapidly rummaging through a bag, pulling out smaller weapons, as if he intended to go down closer to get a clean shot from the ground. But if he did that, he'd be more likely to be seen and start a firefight that ended with everyone being killed.

Desperate, Rachel did the only thing she could think of. She grabbed Garrett's sniper rifle and ran. Her eyes searched the warehouse and the neighboring roofs, looking for something, anything that might give her a line of sight into the building.

As if background music on the radio, Rachel heard the deadly conversation continue.

"Well, actually, I do mind," came the hoarse voice. "But, on the other hand, I don't mind at all taking it off your dead body."

She heard the distinctive click of a gun cocking as she used a small catwalk and crossed to the roof of another warehouse. Finding a ladder, she climbed up to the higher level of the roof. She ran along the edge, looking back at the other warehouse. By now she was on the opposite end from where Dawson and his captors were. Her eyes focused on one of the small windows along the roof line. That was it!

"Please!" came the high pitched voice of the informant. "I was only trying to…"

A gunshot echoed over the line. Rachel's heart stopped. But she kept moving.

Focusing on the warehouse window, she estimated her position and the angle. She brought the gun to her shoulder and looked through the scope. There was a slight breeze from the east, off the ocean. Rachel's hands expertly made the adjustments for windage. She had figured it would be about a 500 yard shot, and the numbers on the screen said her estimates had been accurate. But the difficult part would be shooting through the window at the back of the warehouse. Thankfully, it was still early morning and the sun wasn't casting any glare on the glass yet.

Peering through the scope, she found a direct line of sight through the window to the other side of the warehouse. Just as she thought. She could see Dawson still standing toward the front. Immediately to his left, with a gun pointed directly at Dawson, was one of the men from the SUV.

Rachel emptied her mind of everything but the shot. She realized that the informant was probably dead and Dawson likely would be too in a matter of seconds. In one part of her brain, she was absolutely terrified. But her mind felt almost detached from that. She was focused, her movements steady, confident, sure. She centered the scope's bead on the man with the gun. His side was facing her. He took a small, threatening step toward Dawson, providing her with an even better angle.

"You next?" she heard him say.

She aimed just below the ear and behind the jaw. She adjusted for the downward angle by aiming one inch lower.

"I have the shot," she spoke softly.

"Take it, Rachel! Take it!" came Garrett and Kelsey's urgent voices.

Rachel took a deep breath, forcing her body to relax, to feel nothing. As she exhaled slowly, she focused on hearing the beating of her own heart.

Thu-thump… Thu-thump. *God help me!*

Between the heartbeats.

Thu-thump…

She squeezed the trigger.

Chapter 15

Rachel saw him fall. Simultaneously, she heard two other gunshots. She slowly sank to the concrete. She watched as her hands carefully placed the gun down in front of her. She turned her empty palms up, looking at them as if they belonged to someone else.

What had she just done?

"Rachel. Rachel, can you hear me?" It was Dawson's voice. "Where are you, Sweetheart. Answer me."

His voice somehow penetrated through the numbness.

"I'm coming," she answered, her voice strangely calm. "I'll be right down. Is it safe?"

"Yes, Garrett and Kelsey got the other two men. They're all dead."

Rachel retraced her steps down off the roof. She'd just killed a man. She kept waiting to feel something, anything. But she felt numb, detached, as if she was observing things on a TV screen. None of this was happening to *her.*

As she reached the ground and walked across to join the others in front of the warehouse, several other cars pulled up.

"It's Andrews," she heard Kelsey say.

As Rachel approached, Andrews and a team of agents got out of the cars and took over the scene.

"Nice work," she heard Andrews say. "Although I would prefer the informant to still be alive. Who made the sniper shot?"

"Rachel," Garrett replied. "Kelsey and I had nothing. Rachel grabbed the M48 and took off. I don't know how, but she somehow managed to find a shot."

All eyes turned on Rachel. Most of them were looking at her with respect and appreciation. Dawson was looking at her with concern. But she didn't know why. She was fine.

"Where did you shoot from, Rachel?" Andrews asked.

Rachel pointed to the small hole in the window at the rear of the warehouse. "From the roof of the building next to this one. It's about 500 yards from here."

"Good girl." A smile played across his lips, but he glanced from Rachel to Dawson and back again, as if he too was a little concerned about how she was reacting.

Taking the envelope from Dawson, he opened it and flipped through its contents. "Your informant was an accountant for John Riley?"

"Yes," Dawson replied sadly. "He'd been a loyal employee for years. Awhile ago, he began to become suspicious about some of the accounts. Then Riley began telling him to lose certain files or not record certain things. He did some investigating on his own and unraveled even more of Riley's illegal activities. He couldn't handle it when he discovered the terrorist connection. He had a brother who was killed in the World Trade Center on 9 / 11. I made contact with him a couple months ago. He's been gathering evidence for me ever since. He was very nervous and afraid about trying to remain undetected while gathering the evidence. But he did it anyway. Just this past week, he was able to get everything together for an airtight case against John Riley. He was an honest, brave man, and in my mind, he was a hero. I should have done a better job of protecting him."

"You did the best you could," Kelsey said. "You had no way of knowing his cover had been blown. None of us did. You have no more of the blame than we all do."

"His sacrifice won't be wasted," Andrews said. "I have men already on their way to arrest John Riley. From what I see in this file, he will at least spend the rest of his life in prison, which will be the safest place for him when word leaks out to the public that he was a terrorist targeting his own country."

More vehicles and agents arrived, and the warehouse was suddenly swarmed with people talking and taking measurements. Rachel recounted her side of things to an agent with a clipboard. After warning her that she would have to fill out a lengthy report back at the office, the agent released her.

Feeling the sudden need to sit down, Rachel walked over and sat in the gray Honda they had arrived in. And still she felt nothing.

For the second time today, Rachel wondered what kind of person she was. She looked over at the three bodies that lay silent on the cement. The agents were preparing to move them and transport them to the morgue. She focused on the one she had shot–the body of the man she had killed. Shouldn't she feel something?

Within minutes, Dawson found her in the car and slid into the back seat beside her.

"How are you doing, Montana?" he asked gently.

"I'm fine," Rachel replied calmly. "How are you?"

"No," Dawson said, his tone showing some frustration. "You just shot and killed a man, Montana. Stop putting up a tough front. It's me. How are you really doing?"

"I'm fine, Dawson,… really."

He was silent. She felt his gaze studying her. But she kept her eyes on her clasped hands. She couldn't look at him.

Dawson picked up one of her limp hands and gently held it in his own. Still, she couldn't look at him. "It'll be okay, Montana. The numbness will pass. But you're going to need to talk about it."

A bolt of fear broke through the numbness. "No, Dawson, please. Not now. I don't want to talk about it now." She was suddenly afraid that if she did start talking about it, the numbness *would* go away. "I promise, I'll talk about it later, but I can't right now."

Before Dawson could respond, Andrews poked his head through the open car door.

"We can't locate Riley," he said. "It's possible that he somehow got word we were onto him and is trying to run. We're checking out all of his known property, watching the airports, and putting an APB out on all of his vehicles."

Dawson was quiet a few seconds, thinking. "He has a yacht. I think it's listed under his company, so it won't appear under his personal assets. He could be taking that down to one of the islands in the Keys and making his escape that way."

"If you know where it's docked, go check it out. The man has such means that we can't even guess how he would choose to escape. We just have to check out everything. Take Matthews and Saunders with you. I need Johnson to stay here and finish some things."

Dawson looked at Rachel skeptically. "Maybe you should…"

"Please, Dawson. Let me go with you," she said. She did not like the thought of being left. Besides, right now, she fully welcomed any distraction from herself. "You heard Andrews. Kelsey has to stay here. You need me."

"You two ready?" Garrett called from outside the car.

Squeezing her hand, Dawson released it and moved to the driver's seat, not mentioning another word about leaving Rachel behind.

Dawson made good time to the marina where Riley's yacht was docked.

"There it is," Dawson said, pointing out a large luxury yacht as they exited the car. It was slowly moving past the other watercraft, heading toward the open water.

"It's leaving!" Rachel said.

"Riley's probably on it!" Dawson said with frustration. "He won't let anyone use his yacht but him."

"I'll call the coast guard," Garrett said, taking out his phone. It's possible that they can stop him."

Garrett stepped away a few yards to make the call.

"They won't catch him," Dawson said. "He's too smart. He might be going to an island, but he also might have arranged for a helicopter to pick him up as soon as he's out of sight from shore."

"Too bad there's no way we can catch him."

At her words, Dawson's face immediately brightened. "There is!"

Rachel followed as Dawson ran down the hill and across the wooden planks of the dock. Garrett, who was apparently having some difficulty reaching the powers that be, stayed where he was.

"Get in," Dawson ordered, throwing a rope he'd just untied into a speedboat.

Rachel obediently hopped in with Dawson at her heels.

"This is Riley's boat as well. But this one is actually more Vanessa's than his. Pulling out his key ring, he flipped through them until he found the one he was looking for. "I forgot to give the key back when Vanessa and I used it a few weeks ago."

"How romantic," Rachel sarcastically quipped.

Though she knew he heard her, Dawson didn't comment.

"Hang on, he said instead. "The best thing about this boat is that it's really fast!"

Dawson started the boat and began running it past the docks.

"How in the world are we going to stop that yacht even if we do catch it?" Rachel asked practically.

"Not sure," Dawson admitted. "We should have probably waited for backup or the Coast Guard, but I was afraid we would miss our chance. I'm also not entirely sure Riley is on board. I think he is, but we won't know for sure until we see for ourselves."

"But if he is on board, won't he and his men just start shooting at us if we become too annoying with our little speedboat?"

"That's definitely a possibility," Dawson acknowledged.

This plan of his didn't seem very smart or well-thought-out to Rachel.

As they passed the last of the marina, Dawson increased his speed. The wind whipped back

Rachel's long blond hair and left the taste of salt on her lips.

Rachel shielded her eyes with her hand, studying the yacht as they approached. "If we come in fast, I might be able to jump on board before they even realize our presence. Then I could make my way to the bridge and get the yacht stopped so you could board as well."

Dawson looked at her, horrified. "That's a terrible idea! There's no way I'm going to let you jump onto a yacht, especially when it probably has a dangerous and desperate criminal on-board."

"What is your idea, then?" Rachel asked. "You're the one whose brilliant plan has landed us in this mess to begin with. We can't stop the yacht from here. You certainly can't jump on; you need to run the boat. That leaves me. I'll be careful. I won't even look for Riley. I'll just get the yacht stopped. Aside from turning back, this is our only option. I can do this."

Dawson looked around. The yacht was making good time, and they were already far away from the shore with no sign of the Coast Guard or any other reinforcements.

"Fine," he said finally, but his eyes were still tortured. "But please be careful! I'll never forgive myself if something happens to you."

"Don't worry, Hollywood. I've got this."

Dawson smiled. This was the first time she had used his nickname since she had found out about Vanessa. Rachel felt a little aggravated with herself. She hadn't meant to give him any encouragement. The name had just slipped out.

As Dawson brought the speedboat closer to the yacht, Rachel tried to get in position at the front. She looked down at the white foam mixing with the blue of the deep water and her stomach tumbled. What was she doing? She wished she was as confident as she'd sounded to Dawson!

There was a ladder attached to the steep side of the yacht. Dawson drew close to it. Her thoughts swirled, and her breathing came in short gasps. Was she really going to jump from a boat to a ladder and then climb aboard, avoid the dangerous terrorist, and somehow get them to stop the vessel? On second thought, Dawson was right. She was crazy!

Dawson was able to bring the speedboat so close that it really wasn't much of a jump to grasp hold of the ladder. Before her mind could catch up with what her body was doing, she was hanging securely on the ladder, and Dawson and the speedboat were falling away from the yacht.

Rachel climbed and peeked over the side. The deck was deserted. Everyone must be inside, otherwise there was no way they would have missed the sound of the speedboat's noisy approach.

Her feet padded soundlessly on the deck as she climbed aboard.

She was a Montana girl. She knew next to nothing about boats, especially large ones like this yacht. The extent of her knowledge came from the few times she went on her uncle's boat on a lake in the summer. She had tried both water skiing and wakeboarding. After failing miserably at both, she'd decided to stick to land.

The bridge, where they steered the yacht, should be at the front, right? Rachel walked along the deck, and then crawled under a long line of windows until she reached a wall at the front. Seeing another ladder, she climbed to the top of the enclosed area and crawled around to the windows wrapping around the very front. Thankfully, there were plenty of bars, ropes, and other handholds for her to maneuver easily across the roof.

Holding tightly to a bar, she carefully leaned her head down to one of the large front side windows to peek inside. She could see only one man. He had a clipboard and was making marks as he checked and adjusted some instruments. To her delight, the window was open, letting in the ocean breeze. Over the swishing of the yacht through the water, Rachel could hear the man humming off-tune as he worked.

Finding a secure hold for both of her hands, Rachel switched her position with her face to the side of the boat and her legs down toward the window. Taking a deep breath, she straightened her legs, swinging them out, then in. As she felt them enter the window, she let go and swung easily into the room.

The man looked up, startled. Before he could speak, Rachel had the Glock from her hip drawn and aimed at him.

"Hi," she said calmly. "I'm with the Department of Homeland Security. I'm going to need you to stop this yacht."

Shock registered on the man's face, his mouth fell open, and he just stared at her.

Rachel glanced at all the buttons and instruments that made up the helm. She didn't have a clue how to stop this thing. She was going to need this guy to cooperate."

"Did you hear me?" She asked. "I told you to stop this boat!"

As if her words finally sunk in, the man nodded his head slightly and turned, flipping a few switches and pushing some buttons. Rachel immediately felt their forward motion slow.

"Thank you," she said.

The man, pale and still in shock, stared at her. She stared back.

"What now?" the man's voice cracked after the silence of a few long seconds.

"I'm trying to decide if I need to knock you out before I leave," Rachel said thoughtfully.

He seemed harmless enough. He was probably just the captain of the yacht and not in league with Riley, but she didn't feel like she could risk it. He might restart the yacht after she left or come up behind her with some kind of weapon.

"I would rather you didn't," the man said, swallowing hard.

She didn't like resorting to the physical when someone wasn't trying to do harm to herself or others. It still bothered her about having to use a nerve strike on the security guard, even though it had been necessary and she hadn't really hurt him.

Seeing a rope hanging on a wall, Rachel decided. After searching the man for a weapon and finding none, she asked him to put his hands behind his back. She tied them together, then tied them to what seemed to be a decorative chrome bar running along the wall. While she was sure her knots wouldn't earn her any awards, she was confident that her experience with tying knots and ropes on the ranch would more than qualify her to tie up a man. When she was done, she looked over her work. It wasn't pretty, but he definitely wouldn't be going anywhere anytime soon. She felt rather sorry for the person who would have to try to get him out of that mess of rope.

Dawson would have surely boarded the yacht by now.

"Have a nice day!" she thoughtlessly told the man as she left the room. Realizing what she'd just said, she stuck her head back in. "Oh, I didn't mean it like that. I'm sorry. I guess I mean, thanks for your help. And… I hope your day gets better."

Marveling at her own stupidity, Rachel walked through a narrow hall with closed doors on either side. While three feet from the door in front of her, it suddenly opened. A man stepped through. His shocked eyes registered her presence. She saw him reach for the gun at his hip. Without stopping to think, Rachel stepped forward and, spreading apart the thumb and forefinger of her right hand, she used the webbing in between them in a hard jab right where the man's head and neck connected. As the unexpected blow knocked his head backward, Rachel used her other fist to deliver a hard punch to the left side of his chest, right by his armpit. Finally, with her right hand once again, she made a circular arc, ending with a blow directly to his forehead. The man was out cold before he hit the floor. His fingers had never made contact with his weapon. A mere three seconds after the attempt, Rachel was stepping over his unconscious form. Although he would be out for a while, Rachel still turned around and removed his weapon. Taking out her own Glock, she slid the man's weapon into its place for safe keeping.

She passed through the door into what looked like a dining area with large windows on either side. As she neared the door at the opposite end, she thought she could hear voices in the next room. Holding her gun ready, she swiftly turned the doorknob and stepped through.

Dawson and John Riley stood facing each other, each holding a gun aimed in a standoff.

Chapter 16

Rachel noted that two other men were on the floor of what appeared to be the living room of the yacht. She didn't know whether they were dead or alive, but at least they didn't appear to be threats at this point.

She stepped forward, aiming her gun at Riley as well.

She suddenly became aware of a gradually increasing roar from outside. It sounded like a helicopter.

"Oh, is that your ride?" Dawson asked above the noise. "Sorry, I don't think you'll be needing it today.

As suddenly as the noise approached it faded away.

"It's over, Riley," Dawson said. "Lower your weapon."

Riley made no move to obey. His face was full of hatred, and his gun remained fixed on Dawson.

"You may shoot me, John. But Rachel will shoot you before I hit the deck. She doesn't miss. She's already shot and killed one of your men who tried to kill me today. You see, she's in love with me and would rather be the only one allowed to kill me."

Rachel fought the strong desire to turn her weapon on Dawson. *In love with him? He wishes!*

Riley looked over at Rachel, and if possible, the hatred in his eyes grew more smoldering. He continued to stare at her as he slowly lowered his weapon and put his hands up. Dawson quickly moved behind and handcuffed him. Rachel had no idea where Dawson had gotten the handcuffs, but she'd have to make sure she got a pair too. They would have been much easier to deal with than rope.

Rachel suddenly became aware of another sound approaching. Was the helicopter coming back? About twenty seconds later, they heard a voice coming over a loudspeaker.

"This is the Coast Guard. We are hereby taking possession of this watercraft. Come onto the deck with your hands up."

As they made their way onto the deck, the helicopter was already moving away, having deposited its men. Rachel saw several other boats rapidly approaching the yacht as well.

Within minutes the deck was swarming with various law enforcement officers, and they were moving to place Riley in one of the boats with other Homeland Security agents. Garrett had apparently called everyone he could think of for reinforcements. Even some members of the FBI and Miami police department were there and respectfully taking orders from Homeland Security.

Rachel glanced once again at Riley as he shuffled to the side of the yacht. He unnerved her. For the past few minutes, he had never once taken his eyes off her, despite all the action on deck. He stared with consuming hatred, and it made Rachel more than a little uncomfortable.

As he passed her, he spoke, his words coming in a quiet snarl. "I should have killed you when I had the chance. You have no idea, do you? Life is just a crazy coincidence? That's fine. I have a feeling even mercy has a limit."

Rachel looked at him, startled. Was he insane? What was he talking about?

Dawson was standing beside her and had heard his comment. "Get him out of here," he ordered the other agents roughly.

"Don't worry about it, Rachel," Dawson said as Riley got in the waiting boat and they headed for shore. "We'll figure out what he meant when he's questioned, if he meant anything. It could be that he was just spouting off, trying to get under your skin."

"Well, if that's what he intended, it worked," Rachel said, rubbing her hands up and down her suddenly cold arms.

By the time she and Dawson reached the car, the shaking had started. Garrett looked at her as he started the car. She tried to hide her shakes, but with one look, she felt like he could see everything about her. Garrett was supervising the transfer of Riley and would be traveling back to the office with them.

"I just don't understand," Rachel said. "What did he mean by saying he wished he had killed me when he had the chance? When had he had the chance to kill me? When we broke into his house? It just doesn't make sense. What did he mean about my life not being a coincidence? I just don't understand."

"You may not understand, Montana. There's really no use trying to. John Riley tried to murder thousands of his own countrymen. And why? Money and power. Those were the only motives I could ever find. Any man willing to be a traitor to his own country like that is obviously a psychopath. You can't find logic in insanity."

As they pulled away from the marina, Rachel was aware of Dawson talking on the phone, but she didn't process what he was saying or who he was talking to. Her thoughts were like a ball in a pinball machine. She couldn't focus as they bounced from John Riley's comment, to trying to analyze every event of the past two days. Then her thoughts stumbled on the warehouse. She didn't want to think anymore, didn't want to remember.

"Where are we going?" she asked. "This isn't the way back to the office, is it?"

"No, I'm taking you to a hotel to get some rest. I checked in with Andrews. He'll keep me updated on Riley, and we'll see him at the office later."

"I don't need any rest. I'm fine."

"Then we'll just talk."

"No, I don't want to talk. I'm fine."

Dawson glanced over at her. The understanding and compassion in his eyes was almost her undoing. She didn't want to talk; didn't want to think; didn't want to remember. She closed her eyes and tried to breathe deeply, refusing to acknowledge her body's reaction. She wasn't going to lose it in front of Dawson. She'd done that once in New York six months ago. She wasn't going to let it happen again.

Just keep breathing, Rachel told herself. *It'll all pass.* She kept waiting for the shaking to stop, for the fire behind her eyes to burn out, for the cold sweats to leave her body. But they didn't. Instead, images began replaying before her eyes–pictures of her looking through the scope of a sniper rifle and sighting it in on a man's head.

The car stopped and Dawson got out. Minutes later, he was opening her car door and moving to pick her up.

"I can walk!" Rachel said, getting out of the car. Her body was shaking so badly, she wasn't sure she could walk. But she was determined.

Without waiting for her permission, Dawson scooped her up in his arms.

"Rachel Saunders, you are the strongest woman I know. Please, let *me* carry you. Just this once. Please, Montana."

Rachel wrapped her arms around him and buried her face in his neck as the tears began to fall. She felt herself squeezing the trigger. She saw the man fall dead.

In a few steps they were at the door. Somehow Dawson managed to swipe the keycard and open the door. He sat on the bed, keeping her securely in his arms. She was sobbing by now, her breath coming in short, labored gasps. Dawson smoothed the wet strands of hair away from her face. She opened her eyes, meeting Dawson's gaze through her blurred vision.

"I killed a man!" she whispered brokenly, holding her hands up as if they were covered in blood. "I aimed at his head and pulled the trigger. I killed him! I killed him!"

Dawson held her close, rocking her back and forth and kissing her hair and face. Eventually, her tears ran out.

Finally, when her sobs had lessened to great, dry hiccuping gasps for air, Dawson spoke. "Rachel, you did nothing wrong. You didn't kill a man today; you saved one. You saved me. That man you shot had already killed my informant. He was going to kill me. The gun was cocked. If you had been two seconds later, I would have been dead. Yes, he lost his life. But because of his choices, not because of you. You had no choice. You did what you had to do to protect me and the evidence that will probably end up saving thousands of lives."

"But when I sighted the rifle, when I pulled the trigger, I felt nothing!" she whispered, confessing what bothered her, what scared her the most. "What kind of person does that make me? I shot a man like it was nothing. I took a life and didn't hesitate. I didn't feel."

"Rachel, you compartmentalized. Your brain shut off your emotions so you could do what you had to do. Didn't your dad tell you about that when he trained you? Didn't he explain that you had to relax and empty your mind of everything?"

"Of course he did. But, I never imagined having to shoot a person. He taught me the technique, and I've done sniper shots before, but not like this. I didn't count on the numbness. It was as if my body was disconnected from my mind. I did everything exactly as I was trained to do, every detail. I remember praying, but that was it. It still seems like I should have felt something. That I should have hesitated even a little pulling the trigger. I didn't."

"Montana, you experienced what every soldier who has killed an enemy feels. If they do their job and do it well, they are left wondering what kind of man they are. Are they murderers? Are they monsters for unemotionally killing when necessary? No, they aren't. They are heroes. They are protecting the millions who can't protect themselves. They are making that sacrifice, both of risking their lives and experiencing that same horror you did today. It's the horror of knowing that by doing your job well, your actions took a life, and worse, that in that single awful moment, it didn't even bother you to do so. After the adrenaline and shock, it bothers you. Every time."

At Rachel's silence, Dawson continued. "Remember how I told you that I believe there are sometimes exceptions to God's basic commandments? This is one of those exceptions. You killed to protect someone else. God is the one who gave you the gifts and training to make that shot. Very few people could have done it. I don't think I could've made it. You did well, Montana. Thank you for saving my life."

Rachel's breathing was calm now. She understood what Dawson had said, but it still didn't make the horrified feeling in the pit of her stomach go away. She didn't know if she would ever quit reliving the nightmare, she wasn't even sure she wanted to. The emotions are what assured her of her humanity–that deep down, she was the same person she was twenty-four hours ago. Closing her eyes, she once again prayed. *Lord, help me!*

She was so tired, she couldn't think anymore. Reaching for Dawson's hand, she leaned back out of his arms and lay on the bed. Holding his hand securely in hers, she opened her eyes and whispered, "Stay with me."

"Always," Dawson replied.

As she closed her eyes once again, she felt Dawson's gentle caress against her cheek. And she could have sworn she heard him softly singing a lullaby.

Chapter 17

Rachel opened her eyes to the dim hotel room. The blinds were drawn and the lamp in the corner gave the only light.

"Good, I'm glad you're awake," Dawson said cheerfully from a chair beside the lamp.

It amazed her how the man could get by on such little sleep. He had probably had less sleep than she had, and yet, for the second time today, he was keeping watch while her body completely crashed.

"How are you feeling?" he asked.

"Better," Rachel responded, taking mental inventory of her body.

"Good." Dawson walked over and perched on the edge of the bed. His eyes scanned hers as if searching the inner recesses of her mind and emotions, trying to assess how she really was. Apparently satisfied, he gently picked up her hand from where it lay on the bedspread.

"What time is it?" she asked, searching the room for a clock. "Have you heard from Andrews? Have they questioned Riley?"

"It's about 4:00. It was about noon when we arrived here. And, yes, I heard from Andrews. But Riley isn't talking. He has a lawyer and is refusing to cooperate. They've even offered him a plea bargain if he agrees to provide information about his organization. He refuses."

"Why won't he cooperate? The evidence they have against him sounds pretty ironclad. If they are offering him any kind of deal, he should jump on it."

"I think he's probably trying to protect Vanessa. I've suspected for a while that Riley may not be working alone. There may be another domestic terrorist who partnered with him, but we really have no leads on who that might be. Our hope was to get Riley to roll over on the other members of his organization. But with Vanessa in the picture, I doubt he'll say a word."

"What do you mean? How is he protecting Vanessa?"

"His organization could be very large. If there are other members out there, they will have Vanessa killed if he breathes a word. With that kind of leverage, Riley will try to shoulder all of the guilt on himself."

"He hasn't even said anything about the comment he made to me?" Rachel asked, feeling frustrated with the whole situation."

"No. He won't respond to any questions. He's remaining completely silent, literally. I spoke with Andrews about what he said, though. Andrews said to tell you that his opinion was that Riley was just venting his anger at you. He said you and Garrett had interviewed him and Vanessa when I went missing? He also probably recognized you from when you broke into his house. In his mind, he was blaming you for getting caught in the first place. I know. It doesn't make sense, but, obviously Riley is disturbed, and that's all we could come up with."

But if Andrews and Dawson were satisfied with that explanation, why wouldn't Dawson look her in the eye?

"We need to get going," Dawson said, changing the subject. "I have to run some errands, but I'll take you to the office first. I know Andrews will be wanting to get some kind of statement from you, probably like we did last time when Kelsey interviewed you in New York."

"What errands do you need to run?" Rachel asked, curious and a little suspicious.

"Just tying up some loose ends with the case. I had a few notes I had hidden back in my hotel room.

I need to get those. All the major stuff was in the safety deposit box, but I still need to go over them. I also need to give my parents a call and explain things before this stuff about John Riley hits the media. Then, I'm scheduled to meet Vanessa. She's at her spa right now, but she said she'd meet me at the beach right afterward. She doesn't know yet about her dad. I have to tell her that and tell her the truth about our relationship."

Rachel was quiet. Dawson had been holding her hand for their entire conversation. As they'd talked, he had gently rubbed the back of her hand with his thumb. With the mention of his meeting with Vanessa, all of Rachel's anger and insecurity reemerged.

On one hand, she could tell Dawson was making an effort to be completely honest with her, even though it would have been easier to gloss over the truth. On the other hand... "The beach? You're meeting her at the beach?"

"Her choice, not mine. Her spa is pretty exclusive and has a view of the beach. She thought it would be convenient to just meet her there when she's done. She thinks she's going to nail me down on some wedding details," he said with a grimace.

"But last night she thought you had been kidnapped. Now you're alive and she's anxious to discuss wedding details?"

She called into the department this morning. Andrews told her I had been located and would be released this afternoon after the investigation had been completed. Because we hadn't apprehended Riley yet, he lied and told her I had been kidnapped in relation to my security company. Now I have to sort out that lie as well as fill her in on all the other messy truth."

Rachel remembered Dawson saying that Vanessa didn't love him, that she was not a nice person and wouldn't be hurt by his betrayal. But how could she not be hurt? In a single conversation, Dawson would effectively crush her entire world by telling her that he had only been using her and their engagement to collect evidence against her father, who had now been arrested as a terrorist and would probably spend the rest of his life in jail. Rachel couldn't help but feel sorry for her.

Rachel was quiet as she cleaned up and followed Dawson to the car.

"I'll have the agency put you up in a nicer hotel tonight," he said as they left the parking lot. "This was the only one I could come up with on such short notice."

"Thank you," Rachel said, trying to convey much more in those two simple words. Despite her anger and confusion over their relationship, she appreciated how he had gently cared for her and encouraged her when she needed.

*****

After leaving Rachel sitting outside Andrews' temporary office, Dawson left to run his 'errands.' She understood that Dawson needed to go, but Andrew's wasn't even in his office. And, no one seemed to know when he'd be back. She'd already called her Dad on the way to the office, interrupting him in his packing for an emergency trip to Florida. After her reassurances that everything was fine and a demanded conversation with Dawson himself, her Dad was appeased and consented to stay put in Montana.

Now she had nothing left to do but sit. And Rachel couldn't stand it. After only about two minutes, Rachel couldn't take the waiting anymore and went to find Kelsey.

The thought of Dawson meeting Vanessa on the beach really bothered her. Deep down, she didn't trust anything he said. Maybe he wasn't really going to break up with her. Maybe they were really going to have a romantic walk on the beach while he comforted her about her dad.

An image floated through her head of Dawson on the beach sharing a passionate kiss with a gorgeous brunette. Her dream!

Rachel's agitation increased exponentially as she remembered the dream from the night Dawson went missing. If only she could be there and watch Dawson with Vanessa, maybe then she could reassure herself that her dream and insecurities were unfounded. Maybe then she could trust Dawson again.

A crazy idea popped into her head. Maybe there was a way to set her fears to rest. Her pace increased as she looked for Kelsey. After asking several people, she finally located her friend in a back conference room surrounded by large amounts of paperwork.

"Hi, Kelsey," Rachel greeted as she stuck her head in the room. "Feel like a break? I'm wasting time until Andrews shows up. Do you think you could show me some of the cool stuff they have around here?"

"If you have free time, Rachel, you are more than welcome to help me with some of this paperwork."

Rachel flashed her a look of thorough disgust at her suggestion.

"Alright, alright." Kelsey said, relenting. "You've had a hard day. I'll show you some toys. Both our department and the DEA has given us full access and won't mind at all."

And with that, Rachel's plan was in motion.

Chapter 18

Rachel shifted her position in the warm sand, trying to gain a better angle. Putting the binoculars to her eyes, she scanned the area in front of the surf. The exit from the spa was over there, so that meant they would have probably walked... There they were!

Dawson and Vanessa already appeared deep in conversation as they walked along the strip of wet sand fronting the waves. They were both barefoot. It certainly didn't look like they were having a heartbreaking conversation. But they did appear to be engrossed enough that they wouldn't notice being watched. Not that they could spot Rachel even if they were looking. She had found the perfect vantage point. She was up from their location intermixed with the palm trees that stood between the beach front and the hotels. No one from the shoreline would even see the woman lying on her belly between three palm trees and a rock.

Rachel focused on Vanessa through the binoculars. She really was beautiful, especially with the slight sea breeze blowing her hair and the waves lapping at her delicate bare feet.

There's no way Dawson really wants to break up with her, Rachel thought dejectedly.

Rachel put the binoculars down and rummaged through the bag at her side. Simply watching Dawson and Vanessa wasn't telling her anything. What she really needed was to hear what they were saying.

Rachel located the device she was looking for and pulled it out of the bag. It would have been better if she'd been able to plant a bug on Dawson earlier, but Kelsey said this device would work, just not as well. Trying to follow Kelsey's instructions, she pointed it toward Dawson and Rachel and turned it on. There was a lot of interference on the line. She tried to adjust it like a radio, but there was still too much static.

"I see you're putting the government's resources to good use."

Rachel startled, dropping the device.

Garrett!

Picking it back up again, she turned it off and stood, slipping her sunglasses back in place and wiping the sand from her tank top and worn jeans.

"I have permission," she replied defensively. "Kelsey said I could take a few things and try them out."

"Don't get me wrong. I'm not criticizing," Garrett said, his eyes full of mischief. "If my girlfriend had lied and cheated, I'd be spying on her too. Just out of curiosity, though, does Kelsey know how you were intending to 'try things out'?

"Of course she knows. Kelsey's not stupid. She understands, though I doubt she'll be putting my little secret op in one of her reports."

"So, Kelsey showed you one of the toy rooms, huh? The brunette wig is a nice touch, by the way. You're hot even as a brunette. I wouldn't have recognized you if I hadn't been specifically looking. Of course, it helped that you were the only beautiful woman, hiding out, lying on her belly, and spying on a couple walking the beach."

Rachel reached up and self-consciously adjusted the brunette wig and the hat she'd topped it with. "How did you find me anyway?"

"Same way you found Dawson, I'm sure," Garrett said with a grin.

Rachel looked down at her agency-issued watch. "You tracked me."

She looked back toward Dawson and Vanessa.

"You want me to give you some help?" Garrett asked. "I've used one of those eavesdropper things before. I can probably get a pretty good signal on it."

"No, I don't really see the point now." With a rather helpless gesture, she indicated the couple now embracing on the beach. Apparently, her dream hadn't been so far off after all. She looked away, suddenly not wanting to watch the hurtful truth. "I guess some things don't need words."

"I'm sorry, Rachel. But it's better for you to find out now rather than later when he had a chance to hurt you even more."

Rachel couldn't imagine hurting more than she did at this moment. It was like a knife had been thrust into her heart. She tried to breathe and keep the tears from spilling over. The image from her dream of Dawson wrapped in another woman's embrace seared across her mind once again. A hiccuping sob escaped. She felt a tear squeeze out of her brimming eyes and roll down her cheek. She was suddenly angry with herself. *Stupid tears!*

She lifted her hand to hurriedly wipe the tear away. Garrett caught her hand in his. She looked up at him. His gray eyes were full of compassion and something else.

"No, Rachel," he said softly. "Let me."

With infinite gentleness, he reached up and caressed her cheek with his fingertips, but he didn't wipe away the tear. Instead he leaned in, his lips softly kissing the drop away. Rachel closed her eyes. She felt Garrett wrap his arms around her and pull her close. His lips moved to her eyes, then trailed back down to her ear.

"I can take the hurt away," he whispered. "I can make you forget all about him."

Oh, how she wanted to forget!

His kisses trailed down to her neck, then around to her chin and back up. Finally, they reached her lips, and the passion exploded like fire. Rachel leaned in as Garrett's mouth moved hungrily over hers. Her heart felt like it was pounding out of her chest. The feelings crashing over her were intense, intoxicating, insatiable. The more Garrett gave, the more she wanted. It made her forget. At its core, it was a fantastic, exciting, passionate... escape.

With sudden clarity, she realized what it wasn't. It wasn't love. And Garrett wasn't the one she wanted to be kissing. He wasn't Dawson.

Dawson had been right. Despite everything, she still loved him.

Garrett must have sensed the sudden change in her. He pulled back, still holding her in his arms and looked at her, his eyes still shadowed with intense emotion.

"I'm sorry, Garrett," she whispered brokenly. "I don't care for you the way I should. I can't do this. It's not fair to you."

"Why don't you let me be the judge of that? I don't mind starting out as the rebound guy. You don't have to feel everything for me right away. We already have an incredible connection. I know you feel it. It's like fire and electricity all rolled into one. You can't deny it. You can't say you feel nothing for me. Your kisses show your true feelings for me."

Rachel closed her eyes for a moment before responding. "I can't deny that I have feelings for you, and the chemistry we have is..." she swallowed, "intense."

"So give me a chance, Rachel. Give us a chance. I already feel things for you that I can't remember ever feeling for another woman. Let me make you happy."

It struck Rachel as ironic that Garrett was so easily saying all of the words she had longed to hear from Dawson.

"I'm sorry, Garrett, but the past two days have been so traumatic for me, I know better than to trust any of the intense feelings you stir as being real. I also know that, as much as I care about you, I don't love you. And I don't think I ever can. Not when I still love Dawson. I know what he's done. I know it doesn't make sense. But I am still deeply in love with the jerk. And as intoxicating as it is to kiss you, I can't help but wish it was him." Rachel didn't want to hurt Garrett, but he would be hurt worse later if he held out hope and didn't fully understand her feelings.

"Besides, Garrett, I really don't think you could make me happy. And I know I can't make you happy. From our conversation at the office yesterday, I don't think you know whether you're coming or going on spiritual matters. I can't fill that hole in your life that belongs to God. I can't satisfy you long term. The only chance you have of making any relationship work, especially given your profession, is if you share a faith in God and put him first. Excuse me for saying so, but I think you need to figure some things out yourself before bringing me or anyone else into the equation."

She searched Garrett's eyes, trying to gauge his reaction. Was he hurt? Was he angry? Suddenly, his eyes sparkled and he smiled. "I understand what you're saying, but you'll have to forgive me. I can't give up hope completely. You see there's this one little thing that won't let me."

Before she knew what he was doing, he was kissing her again. But this time his kiss was slow and almost agonizing with its gentleness and… love. At first, Rachel was too stunned to push him away. Then, as she realized the piece of his heart he was revealing, she couldn't make him stop. If only she felt the same way.

"Are you done yet? I'm really rather tired of watching you kiss my girl, Garrett."

Rachel jumped away from Garrett's arms, practically tripping backwards in her haste.

"Dawson!" she shrieked.

Chapter 19

Dawson was standing about ten feet away, leaning against a palm tree and watching them. Exactly how long had he been there?

Rachel's gaze darted between the two men. Thankfully, Dawson didn't look angry, and Garrett, well, he just looked amused.

"If you don't like what you see, Dawson, just close your eyes," Garrett replied.

As the initial shock faded, Rachel's anger rose up. Dawson had no room to be offended. She had every right to kiss Garrett! "Dawson Tate, I obviously am not your girl. We saw you down on the beach with Vanessa. You seemed plenty cozy in each other's arms."

Dawson straightened and walked toward them. "Montana, if you're going to spy on someone you really need to eavesdrop on the conversation as well as watch it. Oh, and it's probably a good idea to watch the whole thing and not get… distracted."

"Oh, she intended on properly eavesdropping," Garrett said, gesturing to the device that still lay on the ground. "She was having some difficulties with the equipment though. And then I came along and decided to distract her. I figured you and Vanessa needed a little privacy for your rendezvous."

Ignoring Garrett's taunts, Dawson turned to Rachel. "If you had listened or watched the whole thing, you would know that I hugged Vanessa in an effort to be friendly and comforting after telling her about her father and the truth about our relationship. I thought she was taking it well. Then she slapped my face. Hard."

Dawson rubbed his cheek. There was no refuting the bright red evidence of a handprint still clearly visible.

"Can't say that I didn't deserve it," Dawson mumbled. "From her perspective, I'm sure I'm the worst kind of cad."

Rachel felt ashamed. She had jumped to conclusions, missing the truth she had come here to find.

"Is she okay?" Rachel asked, still ridiculously concerned for the woman she viewed as her competition.

"She's fine. Murderously angry. But fine. She freely admitted that she was using me as well and didn't love me, but she didn't take kindly to the knowledge that she had been deceived and her plans had been foiled. As far as her father, she seems to be in denial. She thinks it's all some big misunderstanding, and his name will soon be cleared. Me, on the other hand, I'm still a little disturbed about seeing Garrett mauling you."

"Figure it out, Dawson," Garrett quipped. "*I* certainly don't have a red slap mark on my face. My lips are a little sore, I must say though. I guess they just got a good workout."

For the first time, Dawson glared at Garrett. If Rachel wasn't blushing in complete humiliation, she would have glared at him too.

An uncomfortable silence stretched between the three. Rachel didn't know what to say. The tension between Garrett and Dawson was as tight as a rubber band, but at least they weren't coming to blows. If she tried to say something, to explain, she might make things worse.

"So, Garrett, now that you're done with your exercise, I'd like to talk to Rachel for a few minutes. Alone."

"Sure," he replied, smirking. "I'll make up lost time with her later. I've got to head back to the office anyway. By the way, Rachel, the original reason I came out here to find you was to let you know that

Andrews wants to see both you and Dawson at the office tonight at 8:00. He was going to text Dawson about the meeting, but Kelsey hasn't programmed your number into his cell phone yet. And, since she's up to her ears in paperwork for the John Riley case, he thought it easier for me to just let you know."

"I guess he just wants to debrief," Rachel said. "He wasn't around when I was at the office earlier."

"Yeah, I'm sure he wants to follow up on the case, but I think he's also wanting to give both of you your next assignments. I know I'm already scheduled on a flight to Washington, D.C. tomorrow to begin my next case."

"Both of us?" Dawson said, obviously confused. "He's not going to be giving Rachel an assignment. Maybe he's just got a flight scheduled for her to return to Montana."

"No, hc has big plans for Rachel. She's definitely getting a new assignment. He's completely thrilled that she joined Homeland Security. I don't think I've ever seen him so excited about a new recruit. Now, of course, after working with her, I understand why."

"'Joining Homeland Security?'" Dawson said, his voice low and tense. "Rachel, tell me you didn't join Homeland Security!"

"You didn't know?" Garrett asked. "I thought you knew. She had to join when you went missing. It's the only way Andrews would give her any information on the investigation, at least that's what Kelsey told me. She had to sign a contract and everything."

Dawson groaned. "Oh, Montana! Tell me you didn't!"

Rachel was silent.

After a full ten seconds where the only sound was the crashing of the waves onto the shore, Garrett cleared his throat. "I guess I'll be going. The agency has arranged for us all to have rooms at a fancy hotel tonight, so I'll probably see both of you there after your meeting with Andrews."

Garrett, started to walk away, then stopped. Turning back around, he looked directly at Dawson, all teasing and amusement gone from his eyes.

"Just so you know, Dawson. Rachel will probably give you another chance. That's the kind of woman she is. But if you screw up again, which I am confident you will do, I will be waiting. You break her heart, and I'll be the one to pick up the pieces and ensure you never get close to her again. You don't deserve her, and, when you foul up, I'm going to be there to earn her love and make her *my* girl."

"Better not hold your breath, Garrett," Dawson said steadily.

"I somehow don't think I need to worry about it," Garrett said, a strange gleam in his eye.

Garrett walked away. Rachel thought Dawson seemed a little unnerved by Garrett's words, but he shrugged it off so quickly, she thought maybe she'd just imagined it.

"Walk with me," Dawson said, picking up Rachel's bag of equipment and slinging it over his shoulder.

They headed toward the beach. The sun was beginning to set, sending great orange and pink tendrils shooting across the sky. The clear sky above the ocean was darkening, subtly changing the blue of the water to gray. As they reached the wet sand, Rachel couldn't resist slipping off her boots. The sand was still warm between her toes while the white foam of the waves gently lapping against her skin was deliciously cool.

They walked side-by-side in silence for a few minutes. Dawson didn't attempt to touch her, appearing to be deep in thought. Finally, he stopped, walked into the dry sand a few feet away, and sat down facing the ocean. He patted the sand beside him, and Rachel obediently joined him.

Softly, Dawson finally spoke. "I guess it's an occupational hazard, but it's sometimes easier for me to tell a lie than to tell the truth. When I felt it was necessary, I had no trouble lying to Vanessa and telling her I loved her. But with you, I didn't want to say the words. My relationship with Vanessa seemed to cheapen those words for me, because, with her they weren't true. As long as I was required to be involved with her, I couldn't tell you the same words I told her. Because with you, I needed them to mean something entirely different."

Dawson turned from staring into the ocean to looking directly into Rachel's eyes.

"Rachel Leigh Saunders, the truth is, I love you. I'm absolutely, completely, hopelessly in love with you. I have been probably since the moment I first saw you arguing with the lady at the Lost Luggage counter in New York. Everything I've learned about you since then, every experience we've had together, has only deepened those feelings. You are the truth in my life. You are the only thing that's real. Without you I would be completely lost. I am so sorry for hurting you. I beg you to forgive me. Please, Montana, tell me I haven't lost all chance of earning back your love."

Rachel closed her eyes, savoring the sound of the words she had longed to hear.

She felt Dawson's fingers cup her chin, forcing her to open her eyes and look at him. His deep blue eyes were sincere and brimming with emotion.

"I can't stop loving you. Please don't ask me to. You're the only woman I've ever loved. The only one I will ever love. Do you understand, Montana? I love you, I love you… I love you."

The last words were whispered right before he gently touched his lips to hers. Rachel groaned. How could she even compare anything else to Dawson's kiss. There was passion, electricity, yes, but there was also a sweet gentleness. There was love. Kissing Dawson always felt like coming home.

"Rachel," he whispered her name.

Still kissing her, he stood to his feet, pulling her with him. He removed her hat, tossing it down in the sand. Then he gently extracted the long brunette wig, letting it also fall to the sand.

"I like your blond hair," he whispered, pulling out the pins that held it up and then entangling his fingers in the long tresses. "Correction, I love your blond hair. I love your eyes… I love your cheeks… I love your nose… I love your neck." At each phrase, Dawson gently kissed each feature. "And… I love your lips." Once again, he returned to gently, thoroughly, lovingly kissing her lips.

Suddenly Rachel felt her legs swept out from under her as Dawson picked her up and whirled her around in a complete circle. Then he sat back down in the sand, keeping her firmly in his lap.

Smiling, she reached up and touched his face. "You have to promise me one thing."

"Anything."

"No more lies from here on out. No more deception."

"I promise. I won't lie to you again. I'll tell Andrews no more cases that involve romancing an asset. Unless, of course, that asset is you."

"I'm serious, Dawson. I can't handle it if you lie to me again. I have to be able to trust you. That's going to take some time to rebuild. But if, at some later date, I find out that you've once again deceived me? It's over."

For a second, Rachel thought she saw stark fear in Dawson's eyes, but then he nodded seriously. "I understand. From here on out. No more lies."

After the pause of a few beats, he continued. "You do need to understand something, though. Even though you're an agent now, there are still going to be some things I can't tell you–specifically about cases I've already been assigned. I'm sorry, I just can't. But I will never lie to you again. I know that you don't like that I can't share everything about work with you, but you would face the same thing if you were with Garrett."

"I'm not going to be with Garrett."

Dawson looked curious and more than a little unsure. After all, Rachel knew he had seen them kissing at least once only a while ago.

Rachel shrugged and sighed dramatically. "He just doesn't kiss like you do."

Dawson tipped his head back and laughed. "You don't know how glad I am to hear you say that!"

Then, once again, he kissed her. Before she was ready for him to stop, Dawson pulled away, groaning.

"Oh, how I wish you hadn't joined Homeland Security! I knew Andrews wanted you as an agent, but I didn't know he would resort to such lengths. I've been trying to block him for the last six months! I don't know if I can handle having you involved with all this, Montana. It's too dangerous. How can I focus on what I need to do when I'm constantly worried about the safety of the woman I love?"

Rachel looked at him, trying to understand. "Andrews and I figured out you had intercepted his job offers, but I assumed it was because you didn't think I'd make a good agent."

Dawson looked at her like she was crazy. "I knew you'd be a phenomenal agent! I didn't want you anywhere near Homeland Security for my sake! Plus, as an agent, you always see the worst of humanity as well as having to deal with deception and constant danger. It isn't easy. It's not something I would have ever wanted for you. I would have done absolutely anything to save you from having to experience what happened this morning. And, now, since you're an agent, I can do nothing to prevent it from happening again."

"I didn't have a choice," Rachel said. "It was the only way I could get any information on your disappearance. It's the only way they would let me help find you."

"I know. It was a hand expertly played by Andrews. He could have made an exception and let you help out on this one case. He can pretty much do whatever he wants. As you said, he already suspected you were involved in it as my failsafe. But, he used the situation to get what he's been wanting for the past six months—you."

"I didn't think I had a choice," Rachel murmured. "I was desperate. I had to find you. I only did it because…"

"I know, Montana. You did it because you love me. Because despite everything that's happened, despite everything I've done, you're still deeply in love with this jerk."

Rachel looked at him sharply, noting the overly innocent gleam in his eye. Those were the exact words she'd told Garrett. Just how much of the interaction between her and Garrett *had* he seen and heard? She felt her face blushing with the thought that Dawson had witnessed even part of that first kiss between them.

Trying to cover her embarrassment, Rachel leaned in and kissed Dawson. Once again, everything around them faded–the sound of the waves, the sight of the first stars peeking through the night sky–everything was insignificant compared to her and Dawson.

Pulling away just a fraction, Rachel whispered. "I do love you. Madly, deeply, completely. Oh, how I love you, you jerk!'

Dawson laughed and pulled her back to him once again.

Chapter 20

Rachel felt the stares as she and Dawson walked through the DEA offices. It seemed strange that there should be so many people working at 8:00 at night, let alone that the offices should be crowded and hectic. But, since one of the biggest cases of the last decade had just been cracked, it looked as if every employee might be pulling an all-nighter at the office. It was just a matter of time before the news reached the media, and Rachel knew there was pressure to get as much done as possible on the investigation before that happened.

As she and Dawson made their way to Andrews' temporary office, employees respectfully parted in front of them. Many smiled and nodded. Others just gawked. Rachel looked at Dawson to see if he was noticing this. But, the attention wasn't directed at Dawson, it was directed at her.

After leaving the beach, they had stopped at a fast food place. Rachel couldn't remember the last time she'd had an actual meal. For the past two days, she'd just grabbed snacks whenever available. Dawson promised her a real meal at a nice restaurant in the morning, but at that moment, Rachel didn't care. She had been so hungry that the cheeseburger and fries might have qualified as the best food she'd ever tasted. But by the time they reached Andrews' door, that wonderful food felt like it was turning sour in her stomach. The looks people were giving made her feel highly self-conscious. Was there some ketchup still on her mouth? Why was everyone focusing on her? What was going on?

At Dawson's knock, Andrews bid them to enter.

"Has Riley started talking?" Dawson asked, not waiting for Andrews to speak.

"No, and I don't think he will. We'll have to use other angles to investigate any accomplices; we're not going to get anything out of him." Andrews extended his hand to Dawson. "I know I saw you at the warehouse, but we were both rather preoccupied. It's good to see you alive and well, Tate. I had my doubts there for a while. Just out of curiosity, how are you alive? If Riley was on to your investigation, I would have assumed he would have just killed you."

Dawson rubbed his jaw. From the obvious cuts and bruises, he had taken a few hits in that location. "They were trying to find out who else knew. They didn't yet know who I worked for, and they were afraid I wasn't working alone. They tried to get me to answer their questions about who else knew about my investigation. I wouldn't give them any information, of course. But I knew it was only a matter of time before Riley figured out I was DHS. Then he would have wasted no time in killing me."

Andrews nodded, his eyes taking in Dawson's many colorful injuries on his face and exposed arms. "Did the doctor check you out?"

"Yes, he examined me this afternoon. I'm fine. Only minimal injuries that will heal quickly."

"Good," Andrews said, indicating they should sit in the chairs in front of the desk. You gave us quite a scare, though I do have to commend you on a job well done. You practically single-handedly broke this case. But we are going to have to reassess your reporting methods. If Rachel hadn't found that bank security box, we wouldn't have any idea what you were working on or why you had disappeared."

"I'll consider revising my methods," Dawson said. "But I do need to point out that it all worked out as I had planned. I always told you I had a failsafe."

"Ah, yes, and now your failsafe is a full-fledged Homeland Security agent, though I imagine you're not too pleased about that. Speaking of which, we also need to discuss your apparent interference with some Homeland Security correspondence."

"Does it really matter at this point, Andrews?" Dawson said, his tone showing his displeasure. "Rachel is an agent. You got your way."

"Indeed I did," Andrews said, his self-satisfied smile reminding Rachel slightly of the Cheshire Cat in *Alice in Wonderland.*

Turning to her, he continued. "I do have to tell you, Saunders, that your performance on this case has not met my expectations; it has far exceeded them. While Tate's actions cracked this case, your actions saved it. I'm very pleased to see that I was right about you. However, despite your impressive performance, there are some rules we still need to tend to. I am granting you two weeks leave so that you may recover from this last case and put your affairs from Montana in order. After two weeks, I will expect you back in New York for extensive new agent training."

"Thank you for the leave, sir." Rachel responded. "I'm sure two weeks will be more than adequate." She knew he didn't have to grant her the time off, and she appreciated it.

"Tate, I am also granting you two weeks leave. After this case, you need the break. After your leave, you can meet me back in New York so we can discuss your other cases and future assignments."

"Thank you, sir," Dawson responded. "But I also have two other requests."

Andrews eyebrows raised in curiosity.

"A few months back, you asked me to consider doing a round as an instructor in training new recruits. At the time, I said I wasn't interested. I've changed my mind. I would like to take the round of training that begins in two weeks."

Andrews eyes sparkled with humor, and his mouth quirked. "I somehow thought you might have a sudden change of heart on that offer. Request granted. You will be one of the instructors for the group Saunders will be joining. Though I imagine trying to train Rachel Saunders will be like trying to teach music to Mozart, there are regulations that must be followed."

"I should probably just have her do the teaching," Dawson said dryly.

"That's not a bad idea," Andrews said. "And now your other request?

"After you sign off on Rachel's training, I want to be her partner."

At this, Andrews tipped his head back and laughed heartily. "Tate, you're a little too late for that role! You're going to have to get in line! Already today, I've had more requests than I can count of agents volunteering, requesting, and outright demanding to be Saunders partner."

"Garrett Matthews," Dawson said through clenched teeth.

"Of course, Matthews has made the request. But there are a lot of others as well. You see, Kelsey Johnson was recording the security feed last night when you, Garrett, and Rachel had an encounter with some security guards in John Riley's kitchen. She showed the recording to me. Somehow, it got leaked to the rest of the department and even made it back to the New York offices."

By the overly innocent look on his face, Rachel could guess how the recording had been 'leaked.' Suddenly the stares and attention Rachel had received made sense.

Andrews continued. "For some reason, everyone loves seeing Saunders beat up five guys in less than two minutes. It's become quite popular in a very short amount of time. And, I guess that explains the high volume of requests I have received from agents wanting her to be assigned as his or her partner."

Dawson was glowering. "With all due respect, sir, I believe I have earned the right to be placed at the top of that list."

Andrews suddenly turned serious. "You're right, Tate. Until Saunders came along, you were the best agent I had. And with your work on the New York attempted bombing and now your work here in Miami, you have earned top placement for just about anything you want. Honestly, I had already intended on placing you and Saunders together as partners. Normally there is no way I would put two agents together who are romantically involved, and I assume that is still the status of your relationship." At Dawson's firm nod, he continued. "But, I also don't normally find two agents who work so well together. I think you bring out the best in each other. So, I think it's in the agency's best interest for you two to be partners."

"Thank you, sir," Dawson said simply.

A spark of humor lit Andrews' eyes. "I imagine it must be rather comforting to know that if a bad guy is beating you up, your girlfriend can step in and take care of him for you."

Rachel felt heat rising in her face.

Dawson reached out, picked up her hand, and held it. With a straight, serious face, he said to Andrews, "I certainly find it reassuring."

Chapter 21

The sun dipped past the mountains, flinging a grand finale of orange and purple streamers shooting across the sky. The Montana breeze whispered through the evening air, cooling what had been a wonderfully warm spring day. Rachel shivered and snuggled closer to Dawson on the porch swing. Though the temperature was dropping, she wasn't ready yet to go back inside. Dawson readjusted the blanket to more fully cover Rachel and drew her so close she was practically sitting on his lap. He gently kissed the top of her head.

"It's been another great day, hasn't it?" he said.

Rachel smiled. "It's been wonderful. It's so nice that your parents were able to come for a visit on such short notice."

"Dad being a pilot definitely has its perks. But I'm a little afraid they might be having too good of a time. Both Mom and Dad love it here already. It wouldn't surprise me if they decided to sell everything in Florida and retire up here in Montana."

"That wouldn't be so bad, would it? Our parents seem to get along well. And I really like them too. I wouldn't mind having them closer."

"Don't get me wrong. My parents absolutely adore you. And it's not just because they disliked Vanessa and were so relieved I wasn't marrying her. They think you're the best thing to ever happen to me, and they're right. But *I* would mind having them here!"

Trying to explain, Dawson continued, "My parents took the news of me being in a DHS agent very well. Dad said they had suspected for a long time that I might be involved in some government agency. Things just didn't add up. But, them now knowing what I do gives them free license to worry about me and be more involved in my life. I know you and I will be spending time in New York, but we'll still be here between cases. I don't know that I can handle having them so close!"

"I don't know," Rachel said thoughtfully. "Look on the bright side, maybe they could keep my parents company and even have worry parties together."

"You think your parents will worry? Your dad, especially, seemed to take the news of you joining

Homeland Security very well. He's obviously very proud."

"Oh, he took it well, but that doesn't mean he won't worry himself to death. I think you can expect him to corner you sometime before we leave and instruct you to 'keep an eye on me.'"

"Let's not talk about leaving," Dawson said, his lips in her hair. "We still have a few more days to enjoy before our time here is up."

"I don't want to leave!" Rachel moaned. "Just the thought ties my stomach in knots."

"You know you don't have to worry about the training, right? It's just a formality, and you'll whiz through everything. I was serious about having you do some of the teaching. You're going to be phenomenal, and it only makes sense."

"I'm not really worried about the training," Rachel said. But, she was still too quiet.

"Are you worried about leaving the ranch? You shouldn't be. Your dad will have plenty of help. Xavier seems like a really great guy."

"I know. I can't believe Phillip actually did a good job. Dad said Phillip was only here for a day, but he found Xavier and then insisted on hiring him to help Dad until I got back. I'm so glad he agreed to stay on. He's an excellent ranch hand. No matter what Dad says though, I'm going to pay Xavier from my wages."

"So, if you're not worried about the training and not worried about the ranch, what is causing your beautiful forehead to scrunch up?"

Rachel was silent, looking down at her hands and inspecting her nails. Finally, she said, "I'm worried about *after* the training, when we are assigned cases. I don't know that I can handle everything involved in being an agent. I'm scared about it. But on the other hand, I'm scared that I will be able to handle it, that I will be a good agent. And I'm not sure I want to be."

"Are you talking about the potential for deception and even having to use deadly force in necessary?"

"Yes, I'm talking about that and everything else." Although in a lot of ways, she had come to terms with that day when she had pulled the trigger, her eyes still filled with tears every time she thought of it. She never wanted to be in that situation again.

She tried to explain to Dawson. "I know everyone says that I'm a natural at this stuff, that I'm gifted. But being good at something doesn't necessarily mean that I enjoy it. I'm scared that this job will change me."

Dawson put a hand on either side of her face, forcing her to look at him. "Montana, when we've talked before, you told me that you felt God had led you to be in this position. That, at least for now, you're supposed to be an agent, even if it isn't something you ever necessarily wanted to do."

Rachel nodded.

"If He's the one who has called you to do this, then He is the one who will strengthen you, protect you, and enable you to get the job done. He's the one who will make you into the person He wants you to be. And don't forget, I'm going to be with you every step of the way."

Rachel nodded again. "Thank you, Dawson. I just may need frequent reminders"

"Now, enough of that. We still have three days left, and I intend to enjoy every minute."

"You're right. I'm sorry."

"Don't be sorry, Montana," Dawson said, turning so he could fully enfold her in his arms. "I like that you tell me how you feel. I would just also like if you would tell me how you feel about other things too."

Turning his lips, he gently feathered kisses up her neck and softly kissed her earlobe.

"You ornery beast!" Rachel hissed, trying to push him away. "Our parents are right inside!"

"I don't care. I won't be able to kiss you nearly as often as I like when we're in New York. I'll probably have to mind my manners while you're in training. And in the evening, you'll go back to your place, and I'll go back to mine. So, right now, I want to thoroughly enjoy not minding my manners."

His little kisses against her neck tickled, making her giggle and sending goosebumps over her skin. "Hollywood, you're terrible," Rachel whispered as he found her lips.

She knew he had intended to distract her from her worries, and oh, how he was good at distraction! As his lips moved across hers, everything else faded from her mind. She probably would have had a difficult time remembering her name at that particular moment. The only thought in her head was of how much she loved this man.

"Rachel! Dawson! The apple pie is out of the oven!"

At her mom's voice, Rachel gasped and pulled away. Reality came back as if waking from a wonderfully delicious dream.

Thankfully, her mom had just called from the open screen door and hadn't stepped out on the porch.

Dawson laughed and moved to pull Rachel back into his arms. "Come on, Montana, I don't think she got a good enough view."

Rachel swatted him away. "Absolutely not!"

At that moment, Dawson's phone beeped. Still smiling, he reached down and retrieved it from the clip on his belt. After looking at it briefly, he stood and stretched.

"Well," he said, "since you're refusing to let me have any of the kind of dessert I prefer, I'm going to go in and get some of your mom's pie before my dad decides to eat the whole thing."

"What was the text message?" Rachel asked curiously.

"Just work. Nothing important. I'm on vacation, remember?"

Rachel knew that Dawson had been going out of his way to be honest with her and tell her the whole truth lately. Usually he answered any question she asked with more information than she even cared to know. But occasionally, he was still vague on work issues, and Rachel knew these were the instances that probably fit into the category he'd told her about—cases he'd already been assigned that even she couldn't know the details of. Dawson was trying so hard to earn her trust back that usually the infrequent vagueness didn't bother her. At least, she tried not to let it bother her.

"Are you coming? Dawson asked, heading for the door.

"You go ahead. I'll be right in. I just want to enjoy the silence one more minute. I know our parents will want to play some kind of game as soon as we both show up. I guess I need to mentally prepare myself to lose terribly at poker once again."

Dawson grinned, his teeth flashing white in the glow of the light from the screen door. "You aren't *that* bad, but it is probably a good thing we don't play for actual money. I'll save you a piece of pie."

As the screen door screeched shut, Rachel leaned her head back and breathed deeply of the night air. After a few moments of solitude, she moved to gather up the blanket and take it inside. Her hand collided with something hard laying on the porch swing. She picked it up and held it in the light from the window. Dawson's phone.

He'd obviously forgotten it. She should just take it inside and give it back.

But the temptation was too much for, as much as she wanted to, she still didn't trust him completely.

She pushed a button, waking the screen up. Now, how did she view the last text message received?

She pushed another button and waited. Drat! It seemed to be locked. Words suddenly flashed on the screen, but they weren't the words of the text message.

I love you, Montana. Trust me.

Chills raced down her spine. She quickly hit a button to return to the locked screen. How did he know she would try to check his phone at some point?

She sighed and mentally shrugged it off. The man was always going to be somewhat of a mystery to her. She'd return the phone to him and resist the urge to throw it at his head. Picking up the blanket along with it, she opened the screen door.

She smiled in spite of herself.

Dawson loved her. And that was enough… at least for now.

Please enjoy the following Sneak Peek of Book 3...

Point of Origin

Chapter 1

The crunch of leaves and twigs under the horse's hooves sounded loud in the hushed canopy of the forest. She had to be getting close. Cautiously, Rachel urged her horse, Roosevelt, through the brush.

Something wasn't right.

Intermixed with the refreshing scent of pine and foliage was a hint of something else Rachel couldn't identify. It had a faint, almost chemical bite to it.

Rachel ignored the tickle of foreboding slowly crawling up her spine. She was not going to turn back now. That strange light had come from somewhere right around here. Rachel was sure of it.

From the ridge overlooking this little valley, she had seen a light flicker in the afternoon glare as if a sunbeam had been captured by a mirror and reflected in one brief, intense flash. It was over before Rachel could be sure of what she had seen. But she hadn't imagined it. Something had caused that flash, and she was going to figure out what.

It was dark beneath the thick trees and brush. It was so still, she could hear her own heartbeat.

Why was she suddenly so nervous?

I shouldn't be here alone!

But that was ridiculous! This was her family's ranch. Sure, there wasn't another person for at least a couple miles in any direction, but she had spent her entire life on this vast property. There wasn't anything around here that she couldn't handle herself.

There! Her eyes caught sight of something peeking through the trees. It looked like part of a roof. But that was impossible! There couldn't be a house here on their property! She carefully maneuvered to get a better look. It was definitely the roof of some structure. Could it be squatters? Rachel nervously put her hand on the Winchester 30-30 strapped to the saddle. She had left her smaller weapons at home, thinking a rifle would be more practical for this trip. Now she was regretting her decision.

She nervously urged the horse forward, the rest of the building now coming into view. It was a rough-hewn cabin, more like a shack. The metal roofing had been covered with some sort of dark material. But, Rachel saw that part of the material had slipped, revealing a section of bright, reflective metal. That section catching the rays of the sun must have been what she had seen from the ridge.

Rachel slid from her saddle to the ground, taking the rifle with her. She loosely tied Roosevelt's reins to a tree, confident that the big bay stallion would stay until she returned. He was one of their best horses, her dad's favorite. He wouldn't leave without her.

She moved forward, placing her weight on the balls of her feet and keeping her footfalls silent. There were no signs of life as she approached the shack. It actually seemed like a solidly built structure; it just wasn't pretty. The outside was bare, rough timber thrown together in a seemingly haphazard fashion. There were a few windows, but they were high and seemed more for ventilation than decoration.

That sense of foreboding was now suffocating, encompassing Rachel like a shroud as she reached the door. Standing on her tiptoes, she peered inside the window to the right. The place appeared empty.

Rachel put her hand on the doorknob and turned. It was unlocked, opening soundlessly.

The second she stepped inside, she knew she'd made a mistake.

Diagrams and maps covered the walls. Strange containers and equipment lay on tables around the room. Three computers waited in a line against the long wall to her left. It looked like some kind of combination laboratory and workshop. Rachel didn't know what she'd walked into, but she saw enough to know she was way over her head.

She heard voices coming from the opposite side of the building. Rachel backed out the door. She had to get out of here fast. Whatever these people were doing, they weren't going to be happy about having visitors.

She spun, intending to sprint to her horse, but her foot caught a metal bucket by the door, sending it banging loudly across the wood floor. Rachel frantically glanced over her shoulder, seeing the door on the opposite side start to open and hearing sudden shouting over the clanging metal.

She didn't wait to see who opened the door. She ran.

Reaching Roosevelt, she placed her boot into the stirrup, heaved herself into the saddle, and urged him into a full gallop. Trees blurred as she raced through the forest.

What had she done?

Her thoughts swirled in a confusing mess. Escape was the only coherent, driving force. Her heartbeat kept pace with the horse's rapid hooves pounding the ground. Her breathing came in shudders. Had she been seen?

They had to slow as they reached the steep wall of the valley.

Any hope of not being followed was shattered with the first gunshot.

Rachel bent low over the horse, feeling exposed as they climbed. She tried to direct Roosevelt on a route using the trees as cover, but the foliage was more sparse on the steep rise. The horse's hooves slid on the crumbling rock and dirt, struggling to find adequate footing.

Her rifle sat clutched in her lap, but she dare not take the time to return fire. Besides, she had no idea how many were after her. If there had been another way out of the valley, Rachel would have taken it, but this was still the most direct route to get help.

Shots echoed above her again and again, chilling in their hollow sound. But she didn't pause.

God, get me out of here! she prayed as she clutched tightly to the horse and willed him forward.

Finally, small rocks spun off below as the horse's hooves grabbed the top of the ridge. But Rachel felt little relief as they left the valley behind and galloped across the plain. She now realized that she had seen something she shouldn't–something dangerous. There was no way her pursuers would let her go so easily. There was no way they would let her go alive.

If you enjoyed this preview, POINT OF ORIGIN, and other books by Amanda Tru may be purchased from the same online store where you purchased this book. Happy reading!

About the Author

Amanda loves to write exciting books with plenty of unexpected twists. She figures she loses so much sleep writing the things, it's only fair she makes readers lose sleep with books they can't put down!

Amanda has always loved reading, and writing books has been a lifelong dream. A vivid imagination helps her write captivating stories in a wide variety of genres. Her current book list includes everything from holiday romances, to action-packed suspense, to a Christian time travel / romance series.

Amanda is a former elementary school teacher who now spends her days being mommy to three little boys and her nights furiously writing. Amanda and her family live in a small Idaho town where the number of cows outnumbers the number of people.

You can find Amanda Tru on Facebook or at her website! She loves hearing from readers!

Facebook:
https://www.facebook.com/amandatru.author
Website:
http://www.amandatru.blogspot.com
Email:
truamanda@gmail.com

Made in the USA
Columbia, SC
22 June 2017